Scraps

A collection of flash-fictions

Edited by
Calum Kerr and Holly Howitt

A National Flash-Fiction Day and Gumbo Press publication

First Published 2013 by National Flash-Fiction Day
in association with Gumbo Press
Supported using public funding.

National Flash-Fiction Day
18 Caxton Avenue
Bitterne
Southampton
SO19 5LJ
www.nationalflashfictionday.co.uk

Cover design by Tim Stevenson.
Typeset by Calum Kerr.

A CIP Catalogue record for this book
is available from the British Library

ISBN 978-0-9572713-4-0

For Flash-Fictioneers everywhere

In memory of Iain (M.) Banks
1954-2013

Contents

Foreword

Hello again.

Welcome to *Scraps*, the second anthology to emerge from National Flash-Fiction Day. Last year, we brought you *Jawbreakers*, an impressive collection of stories and a snap-shot of the contemporary wonders of flash-fiction in the UK. This year, we have widened our scope to the whole world, and are pleased to bring you an anthology which is even more varied, more experimental and – we think – even more exciting.

In the last collection, we asked writers to provide stories with one word titles, where the word summed up the whole thing. This year, we asked for fictions which had been inspired by other creative works: music, TV, film, art, sculpture or whatever took the writer's fancy. We have not included the sources of inspiration, as they are no longer the point; we just want you to enjoy the stories which have emerged as part of a larger web of artistic endeavour.

There is no theme to the collection, and to try and give an overview would be redundant as it would end up being longer than the stories themselves. So, we might as well stop here and let you get on with reading the stories. We hope you enjoy reading them as much as we have enjoyed selecting them for this collection.

Until next year, happy flashing!

The Editors – Calum Kerr and Holly Howitt.

The Short Tree Has its Hand Up

Tania Hershman

The short tree has its hand up, the short tree wants to ask, wants to ask a question. The two taller trees ignore the short tree. They whisper together, the one tree leaning in to the other, giggling a little, flirting, while the short tree, its hand upraised, is crying out now.

The bridge sees the tree and wonders why it's not allowed to ask. The bridge sees the boatman and knows that the boatman will be under and through and waits for the boatman to pass. I will say something, thinks the bridge, but the house in the distance knows the bridge will never say. The house watches the bridge, for centuries now it has waited for the bridge to take courage, to speak. And not yet.

The short tree thinks about lowering its hand. The short tree thinks about giving in. It is such a day, thinks the short tree, and the clouds agree. Not a day for questions, the clouds tell the short tree. The simpering, giggling taller tree gazes into her companion. It is a day for this, thinks the giggling taller tree, not knowing that her companion is distracted. The other tall tree is paying no attention to her solicitations. The other tall tree bends and sways towards the opposite bank, where something has caught its eye. Trees have eyesight that stretches far and over, through years and through weathers, undaunted by flowing water.

The boatman has seen this all. The boatman knows the trees. The boatman has a wife at home who doesn't like the boat at all, because she knows he loves it more than her. The boatman's boat sways a little, watching the tall trees, the short tree, the stone bridge, the stone house, and the clouds. The boat looks up at the clouds and wonders if, just if, it might be time for rain.

Scraps

Claire Ibarra

My grandfather was a woodworker. I grew up in his old house with its pine-paneled walls, warped oak floors, surrounded by towering, twisted trees. My childhood was permeated with the scent of forest. We lived in sunny Orange County. Our home sat low and dark like a shadow in the bright, clean suburb. The carport had piles of lumber, two by fours, and mounds of scrap, which my grandfather used to repair, refinish, and restore.

His rough hands were a chisel and file. 'You must become the wood to know what it is meant to be,' he told us kids with a whispered reverence. A table with a Lazy Susan, a chair, a framed mirror on the wall in which my grandmother used to admire herself as she passed by. That was before she walked out on her husband and eight children. I never knew her. 'Teak, mahogany, oak, maple, cedar, there are as many kinds of wood as there are people,' grandfather always said.

On Sundays, he was up at five a.m. The swap meet was a carnival, where he collected other people's junk, carrying it through the dusty lot in a cardboard box. He brought my mother crates of tangerines, Captain Crunch for us kids. 'Don't work against the grain. Hardness and fragility vary.' Beveled edges and biting sweet stains, he rubbed at the dark knots of the wood in vain. He whittled a new heart out of a scrap of wood.

Peppermint, Just the One

Beverly C. Lucey

Alexander, age three, unwrapped a hard peppermint from the bowl in the living room. His nana watched him.

'Just one,' she said. Then she watched him build a massive parking lot with tiny cars and trucks.

Alexander's father washed breakfast dishes in the kitchen two rooms away. His mom showered upstairs.

Nana wasn't a real nana, childless when she married Alexander's grampa all those years ago.

But she tried. And her step-daughter both liked and trusted her.

Watching a three year old was a bit boring, however. Alexander's nana left the room to hunt for her half-read novel.

She assumed she could read and watch a child at the same time.

She heard the water in the pipes in the back room, as she searched her suitcase and under the guest room bed.

She heard the clanking of the dishes from the kitchen.

She didn't hear the choking, gagging gasps from the owner of the miniature parking lot. No one did.

Jack-o'-Lantern

Kevlin Henney

Uncle Jack's Halloween parties were a tradition, a boozy institution for family and friends, an excuse to do everything before its time, to let off fireworks early and set the tone for Christmas and the year to come.

'Fuck trick-or-treating,' he'd slur, steeped in beer and spirit, tending the out-of-season barbecue, shrimps and steaks and sausages piled high on the open grill, licked by flames that flinched and squirmed with each drink he tipped over them. 'Beer in the cool box, wine on the table, treats for everyone.' Then in a stage whisper to fire-lit faces and laughter, 'Kids, try the punch — but don't tell your parents and don't fall in the fire!'

Family and friends revelled under awnings and extended roofing Uncle Jack had built out from the house. Each year the patio stole a little more garden. Each year the coverings cast their shadow a little further from the house. Each year the flowers had less space to grow. Each year the party got larger, enough not to miss one or two of its number.

Britney stood away from the adults and other children. She stood away from the light, in the shadow by the wall near the shed and the last remaining flower bed, all that remained of the beds and paths where older cousins once played.

She toyed with a cigarette. 'There you go, pumpkin,' Uncle Jack had said. 'Don't tell anyone. Not Mum or Dad or Auntie Sheila.'

Unlit, unprotected, she breathed through it like a straw. Dry, herbal, stale. She practised black-and-white film star poses, the cigarette in and out of her mouth like the nicotine-stained posters Auntie Sheila used to cover up the walls of the conservatory toilet.

She shivered. Out here in the darkness her white summer

dress wasn't enough to protect her. Uncle Jack's Halloween was like fancy dress. 'It's a barbecue, so dress for summer,' he'd say. 'Family and booze'll keep us warm.'

She looked up at the wall, young vines escaping over the top, pumpkins scowling at her from the coping. Each wore a different expression, but all looked like Uncle Jack.

Britney reached up and touched her cigarette to the flame inside the leering smile of the fiercest-looking pumpkin. The tip glowed. She brought it quickly to her mouth and sucked carefully, as she knew adults did. Dry, herbal, stale. Yet fresh, cleansing. It filled her, purged her. She fingered the torn strap on her dress as smoke passed back through her lips. She stared at the shed by the wall, its door ajar, only darkness inside.

'There you go, pumpkin.' Then he'd handed her the cigarette. 'Don't tell anyone. Not Mum or Dad or Auntie Sheila.' Then he'd left to tend shrimps and steaks and sausages, to tend revellers and music, to tend a party large enough it hadn't missed one or two of its number.

Britney leant against the wall, smoking, unsure of whether she still belonged among the flowers at the end of the garden.

The Lonely Heart

C. Norman

'Dude, I know Jenni likes old movies, so let me give you some advice: stay away from Cary Grant,' said Tyler.

'What? Why?' asked Brad.

'I speak from experience. Once you watch a Cary Grant movie, she'll want to see them all, and eventually you'll get to *My Favorite Wife*.

Tyler ran his fingers through his hair.

'There are some movies you don't want to watch with a lady. Movies that will make her ask...questions. Know what I mean?'

Brad laughed.

'No, not really. It's just a movie, right?'

Tyler held up his left hand, showing his empty ring finger.

'Yeah, tell that to my ex-wife.'

The Spade

David Gullen

He loved the desert, loved the stillness and the parched sky. Loved feeling the sun pushing down on the world like a burning hand.

It was so hot the entire universe seemed paralysed. At night cold stars blazed down with freezing light. The desert was the best place to come for solitude, for regaining lost perspective.

He paused digging, filled with intense satisfaction. Then he laughed, remembering how the spade had rung like a bell as it struck Kaltenbrunner's hypercranial skull. The man had been completely astonished.

And he loved the sand's loose, easy depths. Sand covered everything.

Coffee

J. Adamthwaite

My first memory is of flying over the garden wall. It's one of those memories that are so vivid you could be watching them on film. I'm playing in the sandpit my granddad made me and I see a ginger cat jump over the wall into next door's garden. I know I can't jump over walls so I stand up, drop my bucket and spade, and spread my wings. There's a smell of soil and pollen and I can hear the birds in the trees. I hover, watching the cat slink along the lawn next door.

'Just because it's a false memory, it doesn't mean it's not real,' Sarah said, pulling back her thick, red hair. I watched the muscles in her arms flex as she tied it up and then leant forward on her elbows. 'You've got another reality, that's all. And,' she said, stirring her coffee, 'you're wasting it. Have you tried flying since?'

I must have frowned or something because she rolled her eyes. 'I mean have you tried it in your head? Look,' she said, pushing our coffee cups out of the way and pointing towards the hedge. 'Fly over. Go and see what's next door.'

'What?' I said. 'I can't.'

'Bullshit,' she said, shaking her head. 'Of course you can. You followed the ginger cat.' I didn't reply. I looked at her, all serious with those enormous green eyes, and I realised I didn't want to disappoint her. I wanted her to come for coffee with me tomorrow and the next day and the day after that. I looked at the hawthorn just above the couple's heads, the impossible blue of the summer sky above it. And I floated, just like that, over the table, over the hedge, spreading my wings when I reached the top and hovering there like a kestrel. Next door there was another café with red Formica tables and those flimsy metal chairs, a few people eating breakfasts and some bees buzzing around a lemonade glass. A few beats of my wings and I was over the fence on the other side: the back of the chippy with its concrete yard and huge black bins. A man in a red and white striped apron clutched his chest and slid down the wall, his face contorted in pain.

'Sarah!' I said. I didn't feel myself coming back but I was there with her again, staring into her green eyes with my heart pounding in my chest. 'We need to call an ambulance. The man in the chip shop...'

'I did,' she said. 'Didn't you hear me?'

'How did you know?'

'You can fly,' she said with a shrug.

I stared at her.

She stared back.

'Yes,' she said, pulling her chair back and draping her cardigan over her arm.

'Yes what?'

'Coffee. Tomorrow. Same time. That's what you were thinking, right?' She grinned and walked away from the table without looking back.

The Elephant Is Contagious

Eabha Rose

We all knew she had come to see David. Her face gave her away. Flushed cheeks, crimson lips. She watched through side glances as she sipped martini. She always sipped her drink in a particular way, a kind of attempted coquettishness. I saw through her. Women always do. They are much better at it than men. Men don't seem to notice those intricate female gestures, subtle glances between ourselves as we mark our territory. But then, women are more territorial than men. We are like spiders weaving invisible webs or queen bees keeping their soldiers in line or robins protecting their nests.

She was the cuckoo. Everyone knew it. Or perhaps she was the elephant in the room. We knew she was there to prey on our men, but we returned the subtle game with equally subtle side remarks, admired her hair, her clothes, anything to quietly tell her to fuck off. And she knew this. She liked to up her game then. To make herself that bit more desirable. New hair. New clothes. New breasts. She always arrived with her gay friend, Charlie. She liked to have him by her side because he threw her the most undeserved of compliments. She massaged his ego, raised him to the status of queen. He liked that. He liked to sip martini in the same way she did. Emulate her dramatic gestures. But she played Charlie too. He was an accessory. A chaperone who saw to her every social need. He was disposable. Everything was disposable to her.

She would float in and out of parties. David said he thought she was sweet. I wanted to drop a laxative into her martini, watch her sip it with exaggerated femaleness, before resting her head on Charlie's shoulder, smiling up at him, asking him who was looking at her as she inclined her head suggestively before

18

buckling minutes later on the bathroom floor. 'Ooo, I hope she's ok', I would say to Charlie in the softest most nurturing of voices. 'She must have had a little too much to drink.' Charlie would, in his typical detached way, say, 'I'll take care of my girl. Get her home'.

'You do that Charlie. You get her home.' And with that, she'd be gone. Until the next one arrived. Because you know, the elephant is contagious.

Religion

Paul Kavanagh

0:00: Come on boys.   Come on boys.   God if you can hear me I know I owe you a thousand maybe three thousand Our Fathers   but come on. Right I'll give you one now in good faith   Our Father who art in Heaven   bloody hell.

0:07: Praying again.

1:00: Started but he never listens. I remember I asked him for cancer not for me but for my father he was a right bastard.

1:56: Well.

2:02: He's over there.

13:04: My father caught the cancer if you can catch the cancer anyway he had cancer   wait   no way   did you see that referee   my mother too   strange   she didn't smoke he smoked   he was never without a cigarette   but she she never   no way   did you see that   no wonder he's not got kids.

24:00: Look at them   they're a strange bunch   strange looking.

25:06: They're animals. You know there's only thirty three teeth between the lot of them and ten are false.

26:05: No way   did you see that   I don't believe that   You should give him your glasses   come on.

37:00: We have to win today.   We have to

38:21: No   No   No   Yes
thank you God.

40:11: I only pray to God when I want something.

43:34: Me too.   Look at him   shout something   call
him a name   go on.

45:02: Did you see the look he   no   that was
close.

Half Time

45:00 Why do we come here   we could be doing so much
more   we could be in a museum   in a   library   why   I
bought a book the other day for the wife. I was on the bed
reading the book. Maria came out of the bathroom. She
climbed onto the bed and lay on her belly. She started to go
through the book.
        Look at that.
The God Priapus, I read.
It's huge.
It's to chastise burglars.
We should go to the hospital and find the bastard that broke
into our shed.

50:23: We were lucky there   God please don't let it rain

50:56: No coat again.

70: 34: I love that song   sends shivers   no way   come on
the book.

21

80:35: What's the dirtiest thing you have ever done? asks the wife.

I don't know.

Think.

I did this, she says pointing, it was so much fun.

89:00: We are going down we are going down we are going down.

89:35: Four minutes.

93:00: Corner   yes.   Quick go on. Tell me.

93:03 No   No   he should have had that

93:07: Tell me.

94:04: The Greeks and Romans really knew how to have sex, I tell you that.

94:05: Sounds great.   Tell me.   Wait.   What did she do?

94:34: Greek and Roman Pornography. Dr. Rachel Adams-Smith. 40ft Press. Page 235.

94:45: Our father who art in heaven

94:46: Do you really believe in God.

94:49: No. God's a cun

94:50: Penalty!!!

94:55: Goal.

95:01: We are going down.

Quench

Judy Darley

Dressed in her winter coat and winter boots, Amma feels over-warm in the art gallery, so much so that she considers peeling off a layer, leaving some woollen aspect of her clothing pushed beneath a bench to retrieve before she leaves. The heat is making her contact lenses feel dry and her tongue is quietly, uncomfortably, cleaving to the roof of her mouth.

If she is quick, speeds through the exhibition fast, she'll be able to escape into the fresh air outside, maybe go somewhere for a quick cuppa before heading home. The thought makes her smile to herself as she strides past most of the displays, giving them only the most cursory of looks.

The central piece of the exhibition is a gigantic block of tea, made from countless leaves pressed together – a full ton, according to the literature pinned to one wall. The block is as high as her breasts; its corners are as sharp as teacups are round. Amma holds her face close to it to see if she can inhale the fragrance of tea, believes she may have caught the faintest whiff of tannin, but then realises her receptors are most likely simply telling her what she hopes to smell. The life has been squeezed right out of this tea, she thinks. For all its glossy solidity, it may well be as dry and flavourless as dirt.

Amma glances round quickly, checks that the security guard is absorbed in watching a gaggle of art students in the far corner. She leans in towards the block of tea, sticking her tongue out as far as she can, for one sly, secretive, inquiring lick.

A Canvas, Darkly

Sam E.A.B. Russell

I'm here to see King Charles I, who looks from the canvas in three directions, and am making my way there to the next floor when the crowds, come for temporary exhibitions, usher me into a room. It's a place of contemporary crush; these seas of colour, all black and maroon. A light red above the gloom hovers massive on the wall. 'Have the rectangles been brushed atop the first layer or are they being pulled through?' A co-observer comments to no one, though we are surrounded by everyone.

I inspect the label. Rothko, *Light Red Over Black*.

I look up and see that my face is suddenly too near and in danger of dipping into the paint. There are veils where there should be edges. Unfinished and undefined, they consume me. Everyone in this room is being supped from, swallowed by thin, shifting borders of red. I'm unable to step back without falling into other people. They speculate.

'It breathes, don't you think?'

I think of Charles, disembodied in his frame, and how he doesn't move an inch, transfixed with looking only to himself. One day, that head came off clean. But Rothko has layered a faceless face with eyes that can't fit in this room. Stares in between the frayed rectangles pin and strip me. Charles and his faces vanish into the vibrating boundaries.

I back away into a momentary gap, where the people have clustered together, and slip from the crowds, the enormity of the suffocating gallery, with those devouring eyes on my back.

It stole a part of me, drank deep and quick before I could notice. It was enough to lure me, after I had puzzled at the King's nose for half an hour in silence, to the gift shop. I bought a facsimile of the thing.

I wake every morning, ignore the blinding red and the

compressing spaces of shadow below and search the borders of *Light Red Over Black* for the unknown part of me it took without my consent. I forget about Charles and what he may have thought of as he posed.

contemplating rothko

jonathan pinnock

dyou see angels dyou see demons its the angels i fear most
with a demon you can enjoy a drink and a few smokes kick
back a little cheer on your team slap a barmaid on the butt cop
a feel down a few more drive home fast screw the lights lets
roll and if a few fists fly well fuck em

dyou see angels its the angels i fear the angels lying in wait
when i get in the angels that say you shoulda been working
shoulda worked harder youre late noones going to work with
you again they all think youre a loser your works shit and dont
you know it

dyou see demons its the demons that say its ok youre cool
dont worry theyll all love you one day youll be worth millions
keep going lets have another stay have just one more for the
road dont worry i said dont worry who cares if we drink the
whole night through gimme a light im gasping

dyou see angels its the angels i hate the angels that say shes
tired of how you are watch out be careful shes not satisfied
youre no good for her shell look elsewhere she already is youre
nothing to her youre nothing to anyone youre nobody and
anyway youre impotent

dyou see demons dyou see angels go on tell me what you
see

cos i see nothing

Feed a Fever

Freya Morris

Hope is a virus, an unwanted guest. It'll tip-top its hat, knock on doors, shake your hand and give you a wink. You'll let it in because others will tell you to: hope is a good thing, they'll say. But one simple helix will become two. Its protein coat of sensible-optimism will cause it to go unseen until it's coursing through your brain and invading each and every thought. But you won't see it. Viruses are too small. They live on the edges of life, pulling you apart from within, but holding you together with wisps of promises that will either be broken or fulfilled.

This is what happened to me.

I sat by the lake, my toes tickling the water and wind washing through my hair. Hope was spreading into the creases.

But I didn't look at it –

What if it was wrong? It was only hope after all.

I clasped Quentin's hand and said, 'I can't do it.'

'And why not?' he said.

'I'll fall.'

'No you won't.' Quentin's legs dangled over the side of the verve. His loose curls eased into the wind like floating wisps of black smoke: a warning sign. 'I'll come with you,' he said.

'You won't be able to hold me up.'

A smile snuck up one side of his cheek. 'I won't have to.'

'Quent. I've only just come out of chemo.'

'But this is the best time.'

'How?'

'You'll see. Close your eyes and run like crazy.'

He stood up and held out his palm. His eye glinted and it was only then that I realised that we were both infected, and that his fever might be worse than mine, because our own mortality is closer and clearer than anyone else's. If you slid him under a microscope, you'd see it as clear as day that his cells were littered with viral inclusions, enlarging, swelling and clumping together.

And he was drawing me in.

We were detaching. Cell death was imminent. What chance did I have in fighting it? I placed my hand in his and we stood, weaving our fingers together, squaring up to the lake, pressing my eyes closed to a veil of blazing red.

'You ready?' he said.

I nodded because I was. I was ready to say goodbye to something whether it was death or hope, or the pretending to myself that I wasn't infected with either.

He lifted my hand in his, and with every particle within me I gathered them up and threw them at the lake in front. My soles slapped the water. Wind combed through me. Splashes licked my toes. I opened my eyes and saw. We were running on water. We were running on hope.

Penitence

Stella Turner

I've lost count of the years I've spent kneeling here. At first I tried to make a note of the seasons changing but the long hot sunny days made it difficult. If I concentrate hard I can hear the nuns in the nearby convent singing Ave Maria.

It's not all bad. I like it when the villagers touch my head and say a novena to the Saints. It's the children though. They sometimes put things in my cupped hands. Once it was a dead pet mouse that a child thought would return to life. It didn't of course.

I'm praying that the Boss will reward me with my patience. I tried hard to be good but when Carlotta fell through the wicker chair; I was laughing so much that I failed to see the broom that her husband tripped over. The bottle of expensive champagne he was carrying hit her hard on the temple. Ending up in hospital on her 50th birthday wasn't the intended celebration.

And the time I organised a petition to stop the Easter Bunny delivering eggs. His cousin Jack Rabbit said it was unfair that EB had all the fame when he'd spent his entire life trying to avoid the stew pot, having his paws turned into lucky charms and that illness with the unpronounceable name which would make his eyes bulge.

The Boss raised his eyebrows at my appraisal and I knew it wasn't going well when I mentioned the Tooth Fairy and Santa were next on my list. He said he had plans for me, but he didn't mention stone.

The Veronicas

Ana Martinez

Veronica 1 is still, twisted in her stylised posed to show off her lithe figure and taut muscles.

Veronica 2 leans back, casting a glance over her shoulder. Her pubic hair mocks me.

Veronica 1 and 2 look like my former best friend Kate, now my husband's lover.

Sometimes, I imagine that Veronica 2 is gazing over her shoulder at my husband Mike, challenging him to choose. I expect she wants him to choose between Veronica 1 and 2 but I think she wants him to choose between Kate and me. He chose.

Other times, I imagine that Veronica 2 is gazing at me, jeering me and my inability to keep him interested. Veronica 1 doesn't care.

Both happen on the bad days.

We bought the Veronicas in an art gallery in the Powerscourt Townhouse centre in Dublin. It was a wet, cold miserable summer and all last minute flight options to escape the Irish weather were booked. We spent our holiday money on these naked sluts.

Mike did choose a Veronica that day, but then, so did I. We were both entranced by the power and subtlety of these paintings, of the contrast between firm muscles and soft femininity. He chose Veronica 2, I wanted Veronica 1.

We went home and hung them. We stood back and admired them and congratulated ourselves, feeling like art connoisseurs. He lit a fire and I prepared the food – dinner that evening would be a casual affair on the sofa, tapas and wine. We chatted and played chess. Between moves, we watched our Veronicas.

Over time, we amused ourselves with the reaction of

friends to our Veronicas. The obvious embarrassment of some, moving to sit where eyes did not wander to pubic hair or breasts, made us giggle. Kate came to visit, too. We three drank wine while preparing dinner and moved between the living-room and kitchen chatting to each other. We were old friends. Kate spotted the Veronicas and laughed.

'She looks a bit like me,' Kate pointed out. We looked and joined in her laughter, Mike a little heartily, but I only realised that later.

'True, but you wouldn't pose like that, would you?' I knew Kate was quite modest. She laughed, looking boldly now at Mike.

'Who knows?' Mike averted his gaze and suggested more wine.

After dinner, we relaxed on floor cushions in front of the fire. Kate kicked off her shoes and wiggled her toes, warming them. She looked up at the Veronicas.

'They're quite erotic', she observed. Mike watched her. I watched Mike and Kate.

She grinned. 'Dangerous ladies, Sue. That's some competition to have hanging around'.

Later, after she left, I returned to the living-room. Mike was staring up at the pictures.

'She does look like them,' he said.

'And?' I left the word hanging in the air. I took his hand and we went to bed.

The next day he got the first SMS from Veronica 3.

Egg
Alison Wells

He was seventeen, this David, his hair was a little too long.

The knock at the door startled him. A familiar man stood in the frame. David squinted, shielded his eyes with his hand. The man did the same with the opposite arm.

He was selling eggs. He held one out. It had a translucent blue sheen. It shimmered like the earth from a distance.

'It helps you decide,' the man told him.

'Like the magic eight ball?' David pushed back his fringe. '"It is decidedly so", "looking good", etcetera?'

'The magic eight ball? No, not like that. This is the real McCoy. When you hold it, it shows you your future in pictures.' He paused. 'This is the egg of yourself.'

David found the guy believable.

'How much?' The man inclined his head. As did David. They agreed on a price.

The man laughed, 'I'm David Burns.' He shook his hand.

Later the boy wondered how the man had his name. Who was McCoy and why was he so real?

That night David watched the pictures on the egg. He saw a girl with wild hair walking barefoot on a beach. The next night he saw her again. She was his wife and they had children.

David confided in his parents. 'A man sold me an egg.' His father laughed in that brittle way of his. He was a salesman too. He said he wanted David to join his company. David's mother stepped forward and held her son, fragile, against her chest. He could hear her heart beating and such a life seemed nonsensical.

His mother sent him to the sea. He stood among the flaking dunes. He watched a girl with wild hair stride away across the strong sand.

His father took him to the gallery, to the Exhibit of Held

Breaths; a glass orb of changing colours. People were mesmerized. They touched the orb with awe; they left tokens and offerings at its base.

'Look! Need plus belief. That's what it's all about,' hissed his father. 'And power. That's why I went into Sales. It's time for you to choose.'

Later in the kitchen, David stood looking at the egg. The tender woman and the children had disappeared. He broke the egg into the pan and scrambled it. He and his father ate together.

David Burns had roamed for years. He came to the door that was a door of old, the home was so familiar. He fingered the place where his wedding ring had been. He barely remembered his children, they'd got used to him being on the road.

'I read about you,' young David remarked, 'some guy who died alone in his apartment, years and years back.'

David Burns laughed and shook his hand. 'Not me.'

The kid's hair was too long, his whole life ahead of him, looking for answers. They both held the egg. It shimmered like the earth from a distance, showing all the possible pictures.

Q&A
Chris Connolly

Q.
A. How am I feeling? Okay, well... it's kind of hard to describe, you know? That's why I'm here.

Q.
A. Yeah, I thought I should maybe talk to someone about it.

Q.
A. I don't know. Unhappy, I suppose. Kind of like... you know that scene in Midnight Cowboy?

Q.
A. You haven't?

Q.
A. Ok, well, it's Dustin Hoffman and Jon Voigt, and they're on this bus going to Miami or somewhere, escaping from New York because they're both kind of, like, losers and broke etcetera, and they're buddies and they're looking for a new start and this guy...

Q.
A. No...

Q
A. No, that's Rain Man...

Q.
A. Yeah, where he's... autistic, or whatever it's called. But this is a different movie, I don't think I'm autistic or anything like that.

Q

A. Okay, well Hoffman plays this little gimpy guy…

Q.

A. Sorry, he's like… he has this limp, and he's this real pathetic kind of a guy, you know?

Q.

A. No, that's The Graduate. He's like the opposite of the guy in the Graduate, and he's sick…

Q.

A. No, I'm not sick, I'm just…

Q.

A. No, I know that. I'm just trying to use this guy from the movie as an example, ok?

Q.

A. Ok, so they're on this bus in the last scene, and he dies, and the bus just keeps on driving to Florida and it's really, like, tragic, you know?

Q.

A. No, Jon Voigt doesn't die, he's the cowboy. It's the gimpy guy….

Q.

A. Sorry, the guy with the limp…

Q.

A. Hoffman, yeah. So he dies and the bus just keeps going and…

Q.

A. No, I mean… it's not the bus, it's more the way…

Q.

A. What?

Q.

A. No, it's not a cowboy thing at all...

Q.

A. No, that's not it... not at all...

Q.

A. Okay, forget the movie. Please. It's not about cowboys...
Look, I suppose I'm just, like, depressed or something...

Q.

A. For a while now, the last few months...

Q.

A. No, no. Look, the movie was just... an example. I don't
have – what did you call it?

Q.

A. Yeah, a cowboy fixation or whatever.

Q.

A. I don't even know what that means.

Q.

A. Okay, well I don't have one then – a cowboy fixation.
Okay? I'm just feeling down, you know?

Q.

A. Yeah, well... I guess you need to have seen it...

A Forest of Hands

Cathy Lennon

It doesn't matter which room of the new house I go into. They follow me. In Chiang Rai, before all this, I saw a sculpture in the White Temple. A forest of hands thrust up from the ground, lost souls in hell. It made me shudder. Lately I feel like I walk across that forest every day. Sometimes it's hard to resist the temptation to kick out when I feel their grip. But I do. I abandon my quest and I give in. I allow myself to be caught and I sit down among the caressing palms, the poking digits, the desperate clutches. I try not to think about hell.

'Mummy?' Jasper stands in the doorway, thumb removed from mouth, left hand hovering over his crotch.

I lever myself upright on the tea chest I am trying to unpack. I hobble, belly swaying, across the bare boards towards him, arm outstretched to take his hand. 'Where's Lucy?' From around the thumb reinserted into his mouth Jasper spits a sound that could be anything. I cast a glance into the room we have designated the playroom. She is not there.

'Wee wee,' Jasper threatens. Together we mount the staircase while I cry out for Lucy and wonder again why we'd allowed ourselves to be seduced into buying this lonely old house without a downstairs loo. In the bathroom I position the step and lift the seat.

'Luuucy, where are you?' I sing. My lower back feels gnawed to the bone and I massage it. I pull the cord for the light. The sky, through the antique frosted glass, has turned ominously dark and immediately I remember the line of washing. There is no hurrying a child. I move the step to the washbasin and put in the plug.

Fat drops have turned the patio into a Dalmatian skin. The warm air has soured with the oncoming storm. Into the basket the previously dry laundry tumbles and the pegs flip haphazardly off the line like popping corn. I lock the back door behind me and it's only then that I realize it had been unlocked before. I abandon the basket on the table. 'Lucy. Where are you?' I dash from room to room. The weight has lifted off me and my feet skim the ground. Even so my heart is gripped, squeezed until spots dance before my eyes. 'Jasper, where is your sister?'

He stands in the hall with one thumb in his mouth and points at the back door. 'Hands,' he says.

Images

Diane Simmons

They are pencil drawings mostly – seven or eight of them hanging on the wall above Helen's bed. Some are intricate, drawn with a care that must have required several sittings. Others look like they've been dashed off in a few minutes – the aggressiveness of the strokes at odds with the subject matter. Sophie can't imagine the sittings, can't picture her friend drawing for hours in that anonymous room. Had someone been with her? She has no idea of the protocol. Or of how Helen could have coped with being in there, let alone with being able to draw.

Helen stands beside her, waiting for her response to the drawings. During their short friendship, Helen has taught her so much about art appreciation, but Sophie still feels ill-equipped and unable to find adequate words. 'They're good,' she eventually squeaks. Good? She tries again. 'It must have been hard. I can't imagine …'

'Some sittings were easier than others. But I had to do it.'

'Had to?'

'I couldn't not have done them. And it gave me somewhere to escape to – time to think. There always seemed to be people around.'

The number of visitors had made Sophie worry about Helen at the time. Her need for silence must have been overwhelming. But the urge to draw? If it had been her, what would she have done to escape? She can't imagine that anything would have worked – except sleep, and that, even with the drugs, would have probably eluded her.

'I've done a sculpture,' Helen says. 'From one of the drawings. Come through and I'll show you.'

Silently, she follows Helen to the studio. The room is messy as usual. There is clay dust over most of the surfaces and half-finished paintings propped up on chairs and worktops. Helen leads her to the table next to the kiln and gestures towards a small sculpture. Sophie can almost not look. Feeling tears forming, she swallows hard. How can she cry when Helen isn't? Had Helen cried when she had been making it? Perhaps when she moulded the clay or when she'd taken it out of the kiln perfectly formed?

She forces herself to look properly at the sculpture of the baby's head. It looks complete, perfect, like a baby gone full term. Helen's womb did its job of protecting him when her car turned over – at least from any outward signs of damage. He looks asleep.

'They were good – in the hospital,' Helen says. 'They let me go down to see him as many times as I needed – for as long as I needed to get to know him.'

Orpheus In The Underground

Mark Kockelbergh

On the escalator at Waterloo station I hear the sweetest music. A simple melody. Painfully beautiful. Or beautifully painful.

At the bottom a busker plays the ukulele. He's wearing a pink hat made from the Financial Times. There's nothing in which to collect coins. Around his neck is a piece of cardboard which reads, 'Have you seen Eurydice in the land of the dead?'

I walk to catch my train. The music becomes fainter. It reminds me of something. A bittersweet memory.

I lie alone in bed that night and reach for the memory.

Yes, I remember. The time I said goodbye to Helen last year. In a restaurant beside the river:

'I must tell you. I love you.'

'Don't,' said Helen kindly, 'I'm marrying Simon next month.'

It had been hopeless. A chaste affair, we hadn't even kissed.

The next evening, I hear music again. It's different. Discordant, jagged with broken rhythms. At the bottom of the escalator is the busker. His pink hat is made from today's FT, so he must make a new one each day.

Again the music triggers a memory I cannot place. In bed I remember.

I saw Helen by chance after the night in the restaurant. She looked pale. I asked her how the wedding had gone.

'Simon ended it a week before.'

'I'm sorry,' I lied, 'why?'

'No reason. The bastard.'

She was clearly vulnerable. So I took her to my flat, got her drunk and slept with her. She remained silent throughout. After orgasm, mine anyway, I felt only disgust. I feigned sleep and heard Helen softly sobbing beside me. Next morning she was gone.

One evening I talk to the busker.

'What's your name?' I say.

'O,' he says.

'O? What does that mean?'

'Nothing.'

'Who's Eurydice?'

'Wife. Lost and gone.'

'Where's the land of the dead?'

'Here.'

'The underground?'

'Yes.'

'I don't understand,' I say.

'My lyre,' O looks apologetically at the ukulele, 'it charms the dead. If I play, they'll come. I'll show you.' O walks onto the platform. He strums a chord.

'There. You see?' he points to a young woman walking towards us.

It's Helen. Her face looks like a death's head. I stretch out my arms. 'Helen. Helen.' She looks straight ahead and says nothing. She walks past me, turns at the exit and is gone.

I look round. O stands at the edge of the platform.

'There. Eurydice,' he calls. He climbs onto the tracks and disappears into the tunnel. I don't see him for several minutes. Then he walks back. Alone.

I feel a blast of wind from the tunnel. I run to the edge.

'O. Behind you,' I shout.

He turns. A train roars out of the tunnel, ripping him to pieces.

Later there's a report in the paper. O's head and his ukulele were seen floating together down the Thames. Under Tower Bridge, past Greenwich, into the estuary and finally out to sea.

St Joseph's

David Hartley

He set himself to burying every part of St. Joseph's beneath its floor within the caverns of the catacombs. He removed the decor first, the candelabra, the carpets, the statuettes of the saints, and gave them simple wooden headstones carved from benches.

He followed this with the seating and the vestments and the objects of mass, along with his own sceptre and mitre and all the bibles. With the room clear, he took down the windows; carefully aimed stones bringing out each stained fragment like a fall of winter petals.

An earthquake – a retaliation perhaps – brought down much of the east wall which he set to burying as soon as it was safe to approach. Not long after, the beams and struts of the ceiling failed it and the elements poured in. There was just enough room left below to fit in the roof rubble, but he set a few of the smallest chunks aside to serve as further headstones.

Finally, he dug graves for the congregation who had slumped into their decays, patiently awaiting the completion of his project. Flakes of flesh fell from bones as he carried each body to its designated place, the name of each parishioner etched on the front of his mind, slipping out of his lips and into the howl of the wind. He whispered each one into their rest, inventing new prayers and folding them into simple, brief, painless eulogies. He left the graves unmarked.

Only the bell tower remained so he shut himself in there and watched the sky. And, with silence and grace, with patience and defiance, with crumbled hands and a quivering neck, he awaited a response.

It came soon after.

The Paper Oak

H. Anthony Hildebrand

FADE IN:
EXT. SUBURBAN HOUSE — DUSK

(Note: the choice of suburban house to be used for this shot is crucial. It should convey a precise sense of normality, but with trans-Atlantic crossover appeal — ideally the exact mid-point between the sprawling two storey weatherboard residence featured in the 1991 comedy hit DON'T TELL MOM THE BABYSITTER'S DEAD (remember Keith Coogan, as KENNY CRANDELL, sitting with his pals atop the roof of the building's classic American veranda, taking advantage of the titular babysitter's demise to get in a little DIY clay pigeon shooting practice? Except instead of the standard inverted saucers, made from a mix of pitch and pulverized limestone rock, regularly employed to stand in for live birds, he uses household crockery - actual saucers! 'The dishes are DONE, man,' he states emphatically. The humour here derives from the unusual usage of the word 'done'; it would normally imply that the dishes had been washed and/or dried - not blasted to pieces by a powerful shotgun!) and a standard two-up two-down south London Edwardian terrace.

If possible there should be a front yard with a large oak or elm tree sited prominently therein; draped over the boughs of the oak or mighty elm (state tree of Massachusetts) should be a large quantity of what looks, at first glance, like streamers or ribbons; on second glance like toilet paper hurled by drug and booze-crazed anti-social teens; and on third glance, on really close inspection, like what they are: itemised receipts detailing a lifetime's worth of extravagant overspending and profligacy, on items as ludicrous as solid gold Xbox controllers, caviar-filled tanning beds, and life-sized replicas of Cold War-era Intercontinental Ballistic Missiles (ICBMs). Who is responsible for such wanton wastefulness? And who would want to expose such a spendthrift? Such is the mystery of 'the paper oak' (or elm).

The house itself should project an aura of dread; without using any expensive lighting effects, it should seem to glow with menace and hostility, while simultaneously appearing warm and hospitable. This dichotomy should be immediately obvious – we want the average viewer to think, 'Gee, I wouldn't mind knocking on that front door to ask for a cup of sugar and then re-gretting that I'd done so.'

Every single surface of the house's exterior should be glistening with slick, fresh human blood, and through each window should clearly be visible the silhouette of a MANIACAL SURGEON, scalpel in hand, cackling hysterically over a recently dismembered corpse.)

MAN (O.S.)
Honey, I'm home!

FADE OUT.

The Art of the TV Chefs

Becky Tipper

It was just a couple of weeks after he died. My mother and I were watching Heston Blumenthal.

'It's a work of art really, some of this,' she said. 'On MasterChef the other week they did a roasted quail, poor thing, balanced on this fiddly little basket made of sugar. Beautiful. Although you wouldn't want to eat it.'

'Yeah, it's pretty amazing,' I said.

'Except that Nigella. Hers always looks a mess.'

'Maybe that's the art of it for her – looking like you didn't try to make it artful.'

'Hmm,' she said.

Heston was making goose livers suspended in a golden jelly – tiny, disembodied organs floating like something from a medical museum, or a dream. He was explaining the technicalities of gelatine.

'I never knew that,' my mother said with wonder, 'that gelatine was made out of bones.'

'Of course,' I said. 'You really didn't know that?'

When I looked over, she was frowning. I wondered if I'd been too short with her. 'Are you all right, Mum?'

'Just thinking,' she said, 'we could have made a jelly out of your dad, couldn't we?'

And then suddenly she was crumpled, laughing and pummelled by waves of hysteria, her eyes and mouth twisted and spasmed, crying with the very thought of it.

She laughed for about five minutes.

'I'm sorry,' she gasped, 'it just tickled me.'

'Are you sure you're all right?'

She nodded and sighed. 'Your dad always did love a jelly though.'

When I went over to stay with her the next weekend, she'd

made one. I found it in the fridge, shuddering with the aftershock as I pulled the door open. It was in the shape of a rabbit, shimmering and tangerine. It stared out blindly from among the half-tins of things, a small bottle of milk, a withered cucumber and a Sainsbury's ready meal. Around the edge of it were delicate swirls of piped cream and sparkly hundreds and thousands.

'What's this jelly?' I said.

'It got me thinking about them, the other night,' she said. 'I thought we could have it after tea tomorrow.'

'You didn't make it out of his ashes, did you?'

She grinned. 'Your old mum's not lost it yet, sweetie.'

That night, when I couldn't sleep, I went downstairs for a drink. From the hall, I could see the fridge door was open and that my mum was standing there in the glow – the way they always show Nigella slinking back to finish off the leftovers. I was going to ask her what she was doing but she seemed totally absorbed, like she wouldn't even hear me. I watched her; watched the flash of the spoon as she reached in and ate it bit by bit, spoonful by spoonful. She closed her eyes as she tasted, savouring each orange mouthful. And every time she sliced the spoon into it she was so delicate, almost apologetic, as if the thing was alive and she didn't want to hurt it.

Bright New Morning

Joanna Campbell

My auntie packed up her hairdresser's scissors and the little soft brush for whisking clients' necks. 'I'm too old,' she said and laughed like she does, her small head tilted and her beautiful new teeth bared like the mouth of a skull.

'You're not old,' I said, frightened by age. I knew she was crumbling, her bones like table-legs chewed by a puppy. A few more flakes of sawdust fall every day, she would say, smiling and tapping her Consulate on the edge of the ash-tray.

She kept magazines on a low table and biscuits in a tartan tin. In the sideboard, chocolate bars were stacked in a blinding purple foil ingot. I wondered if it always sat in there, waiting for me.

Auntie was once a hair model. She had a collection of pictures, so sharp I could see every shaped wisp. Silvery waterfalls, mythical tendrils, sleek mushroom caps. Every fashion, every style. Milky blonde, like silk skeins on a haberdashery counter, too flawless to touch, to unravel.

Now her sparse tobacco-juice hair was stripped by time. It reminded me of our lawn at the end of a long summer of penalties struck into the silver-birches and thumping feet from a swing left keening. The grass was packed down, pounded to iron-hard earth with brave brown tufts.

One day she said she had thrown the photographs in the fire.

'No, not really?' I wailed, wanting to trace my finger round the thick wavy edges of the scalloped card.

She laughed and said everything had its own time.

'Let's read,' she said.

We put our feet up on the pouffe, my small punched-pattern sandals sinking in beside her red leatherette slippers. She took out a Consulate and read Woman aloud. 'Common errors with emery-boards', the article was called. How to file nails without the rough see-saw motion so many girls used.

'People go at it hammer and tongs,' Auntie said. 'Patience, one sweep at a time, is the key.'

And she showed me her sea-shell nails with their skin of pale polish. If I concentrated on them, not the mottled wet sand colour of her dear hands, I could see my young auntie living on and on.

We saw the Consulate advertisement in the magazine. 'Cool as a mountain stream', it said above the picture. 'Bright New Morning', it told us. And how the white minty cigarettes would give you great breaths of the country, wherever you were.

'I'd like to be the girl wading in the brook. Look at all that green. And the sun flickering through,' my auntie said as the bus hissed through the puddles on the main road running past her front-room window.

She replaced her cigarette in the packet. She never lit them anymore. She said they might not have real mountain air inside.

I reached up to pat her head, soft as half-blown dandelion-clock.

'They were wigs for a time, you know,' she said, glancing at the fire. 'No one knew.'

Aspirations to Anonymity

James Coates

The door opens, and I look up as the customer enters. It is the eyes which capture my attention first; pupils so wide that it is easy to believe they have spent their whole life staring into darkness. Their immense depth is contrasted by a messy tangle of wispy grey hair, which floats about, seemingly oblivious of style or fashion.

Age? I can't guess, the hair tells me sixty, while the full, pouting lips shout sixteen.

Gender? I'm too polite to make assumptions.

'Why does everyone, always, do that?' The sulky tone solves the paradox of age; young then.

'Do what?' I reply without thinking. Although now I'm self conscious, and look back to the stack of puzzles I was pricing.

'Stare, stare, bloody stare!' The figure moves away from the door, and steps further into my shop. 'Where's your jewellery?'

I point.

And find myself staring again. I can't help it. Everything is wrong; the attire, the posture, the expression. The person is a collection of innocuous parts, somehow held together by a magnetic intensity bordering on anger. It's a man, I'm sure. But, the jewellery request confuses me. Fascinated, I watch as delicate fingers rifle through my selection of cast outs and donations.

'Were you, after anything specific?' Belatedly, I remember my half-day of customer service training.

'Yes, a ring.'

The fingers continue their search.

'For...?' I let the question hang, hoping for a response that will finally resolve the gender enigma.

'Someone read me a book at the orphanage once, when I was younger, when people still pretended to care. It was about some small chap, and a bunch of dwarves going off to fight a dragon.' The words come from a mouth distracted by the repetition of placing each ring onto a slender index finger. 'There was a wizard, too. The author who wrote it lived near here. After he died it went missing. So, every jumble sale, car boot, charity shop I always go, hoping to find it...'

'Find what?'

'That ring, from the book. It's real! The one that makes you -'

Quite suddenly my customer is gone.

Vanished.

And instead of watching dandelion tufts of grey hair, I'm looking out through my slightly smeared windows at the number three bus disgorging its passengers onto the pavement outside.

I know my mouth is hung open. Wide. And I feel my hands shaking; twitching in time to the erratic rhythm of my chest, tapping out a hollow beat against the side of a cardboard puzzle box.

A disembodied voice breaks through my shock. 'It's what I've always wanted, to walk down the street without being stared at. To hide from the looks and the muttered questions. Do you know how difficult it is to be me?'

The question hangs in the air as the shop door is opened. Only, I can't see anyone there. But that doesn't stop me shouting. 'Oi! You haven't paid for that! It's precious.'

Finding *Trainspotting*

Clare Kirwan

The borrower says to the library assistant: Have you got *Trainspotting* by Irvine Welsh? You know: Choose life?

I'll look it up on system, the library assistant makes it sound like a giant supercomputer, chooses Search. Yes we have a copy. I'll show you where it is.

There's no need, says the borrower. I'll find it myself.

That's what I'm here for, snaps the library assistant. This has never occurred to the borrower, who follows her past New and Popular to the general fiction.

The thing I have against Irvine Welsh, says the library assistant, is that he wrote a book called *Glue*. I wanted to write a book called *Glue* myself. I feel better qualified: I wrote a poem called 'Glue'. I worked in a glue factory. I fell in love with the scientist who made the glue. It's all in the poem, but there's more I could write... a whole novel. The perfect title for the novel is *Glue*.

You've written a book?

The assistant doesn't answer, marches along the stacks: A-C, D-G, H-L, M-R.

Can't there be two books with the same name? asks the borrower and the assistant glowers like it's the stupidest question ever.

That's not the point.

The borrower stares at the library assistant, not knowing what to say.

S-Z. Handbrake turn.

The library assistant points accusingly at a lower shelf.

Here. Here are all of Irvine Welsh's fucking books.

Why Do Fools Fall in Love

Brendan Way

'Barbara?'

'Yes, dear?'

'Why did we fall in love?'

'Oh, because we were young and naive. We didn't know any better back then. We thought you stayed with the first person you met and were together forever.'

'Huh... Why did we get married then?'

'Well, by then, we were a little bit older, but none the wiser, I suppose. It seemed like the logical thing to do - it had been a couple of years after all. Besides, we had a child on the way.'

'Of course. What about now though? The kids have left and it's been forty-plus years. Why are we still together now?'

'I guess because we've been a couple so long, we can only remember the good times. Then there's the factor of age. At this point in life, it's inconceivable to imagine being with someone else.'

'Ah. That makes sense. Thanks, Barbara.'

'No problem, Alan.'

...

'Barb?'

'Yes, Alan?'

'I love you.'

'I know you do, dear, I know.'

In a Moment

Shelley Day Sclater

In a moment they would carry her down. He waits, fists clenched in his pockets, has not offered to help. He hears them moving around upstairs, two pairs of feet pressing on floorboards, moving into position, assessing the best way. Men's voices, low, respectful; he can't make out any words.

Before, he'd been biting the inside of his lip and now the fresh metallic taste of blood seeps onto his tongue, almost sweet. He sucks, keeps on sucking, keeping the wound alive, tasting his own life.

In a moment they would open the door. One of them backing out, a silently agreed positioning, a single nod in his direction, eyes cast down. He sucks some more, the blood flowing.

Here they come. The door can't wait to shut behind them, it's sliding across the landing carpet, then click, click, it's closed.

He cups his hands across his face, as though in prayer, but no prayer comes. He cups his hands to his face, breathes in the smell of common soap; small breaths, shallow and fast. Then it's Mamgu's lavabread, Bara Brith, coal smoke, heather on the mountain, the pit dust stuck to the rough clothes of the men as they clack clack on and up the hill.

And there he is, a boy again, running along beside his grandfather, the wind in his hair, the smell of evening sinking down from the mountain. And Mamgu, always, standing at the gate, waiting, waving. The last few yards and he throws himself towards her, his arms reaching out, her arms encircle him as he buries his face deep in her skirts and, with every tight breath, he takes in the smell of her.

The stairs creak now, one by one, as they descend. He waits, his back against the wall. He breathes in the smell of linseed oil, of brass polish, carpet cleaner, floor cleaner, he breathes in anything but her as they carry her out and autumn blows quietly in through the open door.

In a moment he will bolt the door.

Shoes

Jenn Ashworth

We lived in a big house in the countryside. This was years ago now though – back when we kids still had Rochdale accents and there were deer in the woods in the garden.

Dad was at work, mostly. There were traces of him. Every morning was a jigsaw. We tried to piece together where he had been in the short hours he was home (after bedtime, and before getting up). A banana peel on the breakfast bar. Hairs from the shaving brush on the soap. That sort of thing. Mum used to clean the signs away before we could find them, and in that way it was like a race: trying to find his smell on the pillow before she beat the bed into tidiness.

She was tidy. Used to make him leave his shoes on the porch, in case he tramped muck into her carpet. I saw Uncle Paul once, driving up in the van. He clocked Dad's shoes, gave me a wave, and reversed out again, without stopping to knock at the door.

The Meaning of Life

Bart Van Goethem

Surrender.

The Man with Hands Amid the Rich Tea

Cathy Bryant

They'd worked in the same biscuit factory but at different times, and talked in diagonals.

'Remember Russell?' asked Jess.

'Russell....Russell...' pondered Julie, like a 1970s Music and Movement class about trees.

'You know - Russell,' said Jess. 'With the hands.'

I pictured crowds of Russells flocking somewhere, with no hands, and only one Russell standing alone (probably outcast by the herd), fully-fingered.

'Oh Russell!' said Julie. 'Yes! I started off on Penguins, but he used to corner me in the lift. He chased me round so much that I had to move to Family Circle.'

And they carried on reminiscing and I felt like Alan Bennett, but also wanted them to be angrier about Russell's sexual harassment.

'And then,' said my best friend later, 'You rushed home to tell all your middle class friends about it.'

He was right. Blushing, I reached out a hand for a comforting Viscount.

The Almond Crumb Sofa

Tim Stevenson

'It was like being at war, I suppose,' the Professor said.

He relaxed deeper into his red leather armchair and sipped his brandy in the candlelight.

His wife raised an eyebrow and stuck the poker into the remains of the fire before retrieving her cup of tea.

'Not battles. Not soldiers in the trenches. That's not what I mean.' He stared at the last flames in the hearth.

'It was a race to be the first,' he began again. 'The speed of sound, the moon landing, you know the kind of thing.'

'The atom bomb?' she asked.

'Precisely,' he replied.

She knew not to pry any further. He'd always known how to keep a secret. All she knew was that deep in the Atacama Desert was a machine and it had kept her husband from her.

'It was difficult,' he said at last.

'The work?'

'Missing you.'

She reached across the gap between them and gently squeezed his hand.

'Not being able to call, not even being allowed to write a letter, that was the hardest thing to stomach.'

His wife closed her eyes and let him talk. Four years of pent up thoughts rolled across the carpet.

'I wondered if you'd changed,' he said. 'I had your photograph by my bed and wondered if you'd cut your hair or decided on a new favourite dress. It was hard to remember you.'

She put her hand up to her curls and ran her hand through the auburn and the grey.

'It's strange how some things are hard to recollect, the little details,' he said. 'But that place we used to go to for tea on the square, the rickety tables and the homemade cakes, as clear as day. I used to dream about it.'

'And the sofa by the fire,' she said.

In the deep orange glow her husband smiled.

'Yes, all those crumbs under the cushions,' he said. What were they? Coconut? Banana bread?'

'Almonds,' she said.

'Oh yes. Crushed almonds, that wonderful smell.'

Her husband had come home early. Homesickness he'd said, but she suspected.

'I love you Julie,' he said.

She turned to face him. 'Judith,' she said.

ipping

McNamara

Her eyes twinkle as she takes the apple pie from the oven. It's a surprise for her handsome new husband. He tells all his friends about how well she bakes.

She can see the beach through the kitchen window and knows by the rising tide that the harbour will soon be full enough for him to take the boat in. Some days the tide rises so much that she is afraid it will come right into the kitchen and carry her away.

The back door slams shut. She smoothes out her apron and smiles shyly. But instead of her young spouse, an old man stands facing her, an old man who hasn't fished the bay for nearly twenty years.

Her smile falters as he reaches out to her.

'Margaret,' he says quietly. 'Do you know that's the third apple pie you've made today?'

Their frightened eyes lock and the pie dish slips from her trembling fingers and shatters.

Exile

R.M. Kealy

It was his wife's ring, he was sure of it.

Even from across the road, through the heavy traffic and driving London rain, he was sure. He knew its shape; he knew the hand wearing it.

The flowing traffic came to a reluctant stop and he found himself moving with the crowds, propelled across the road and towards the photograph. As he drew closer to the newspaper cart, he could make out the headline above; 'Record-Breaking Diamond Seized By Bailiffs'.

It was a teardrop shape, the ring. His wife's choice, like most things. He hadn't been so sure, couldn't help but think there was something a little sad about the idea.

He pulled his collar up against the wind and stared at the image below the angry black headline. The platinum band was plain, so as to emphasise the large, flawless diamond it carried. It had been a special order, too big for Irish jewellers to carry.

He squinted at the photograph, blinking through the raindrops. Her alabaster hand was as delicate as ever, wilting under the weight of the ring. He clenched his jaw as he thought of her small hand enveloped in his, wincing at the memory of her impossibly soft skin. He hadn't spoken to her in a long time, much less touched her.

'Paper for ya mate?'

The paper-seller looked questioningly at the well-dressed, middle-aged man who was staring blankly at the display. He wondered if he had had an early drop.

'What? No. Thanks.' He knew the story well enough, didn't need to pay a pound to read it.

'Suit yourself sir', the paper-seller turned back to his slow amble around the cart, proffering rain-speckled pages to the passing crowds.

Suddenly his phone burst into song, its tinny tune fighting

to be heard from the depths of his pocket. He pulled it out, held it aloft to locate the red button, and jabbed it hard, twice. The first to silence it, the second to kill it.

He didn't have to look at the number to know who it was. It wouldn't be the owner of the small, soft hand. It would be a tabloid hack clamouring for a comment on today's story. With no soundbite, they'd just report the foreign ringtone, salaciously rehashing every detail of his downfall.

He noticed with a start that he wasn't alone by the newspaper cart. There was another grey-haired man, similarly dressed in a greatcoat and flat cap standing by his side, focused on the photograph ahead.

They nodded to each other, these men, silent recognition registering on their lived-in faces as they acknowledged shared pasts, shared mistakes. They had moved in the same circles once upon a time. The same private clubs, the same exclusive restaurants and finally, the same bankruptcy court.

They both stood quietly, each lost in their own thoughts, staring at the papers as if wishing them away. Then the other man offered the comfort only a fellow Irishman can.

'Pint?' he said.

Elsie Manor

Kylie Grant

On the morning Elsie Manor's body was found spread-eagled in a small disused boat I woke to heavy rain on the water. The deep sounds rose up until there was no room left to breathe, no space for me at all, and I was forced to open the window wide to let the wind dance around the bed.

I live in one of the few houses right on the mouth of the harbour, a house which appears to be half submerged, the foundations built into the moving silt. It is a house built to welcome the boats in. It was my mother's originally, before she decided to flee the weightlessness she felt whenever she looked out of a window.

I wasn't the one who found Elsie, although the boat was anchored only a few metres from my house. It was one of the fishermen. They say she was found in the early hours of the morning covered in tiny droplets of water from the mist. She had killed herself, of course. No murderers in this town, discounting the sea and a tourist who accidently drowned his wife in its depths while he was asleep.

Two deep slashes on both wrists. Elsie's blood pooled inside the boat, rust red stained the rotting brown of the wood. She looked at peace, the fisherman is believed to have told her mother.

What I have told no one, not even when I've been asked, is that I saw Elsie on the night she died. I watched as she swam out to the boat, the boat that once belonged to my brother and I. We used it to catch crabs in the summer, hauling them over the sides, their claws lifting, saluting the salty air.

In the moonlight I watched as Elsie Manor climbed into the boat and bled to death. The boat rose and fell, rose and fell, until I could watch no longer.

As children, Elsie and I often gazed at each other from the

windows of our houses. She lived in the Queen's Hotel, which stood on the opposite side of my house; the land side. The stable side. I liked it better to stare out at that side.

During school holidays we watched each other eat lunch. She would eat slowly, carefully. Elsie once took two hours to eat a sandwich. Afterwards, she held the empty plate up to the window and smiled as she did so, a wide smile that made her eyes become so small you could barely tell she had eyes at all.

I know she saw me that night because halfway to the boat she stopped, raised her hand and waved to me.

My house is the one that guides people home. The house that watches and waits, that speaks to the sea. My house and I waved to Elsie that night, guiding her onwards. We whispered to her over the waves, close your eyes, we said. Close your eyes.

The Warden

Thaddeus Howze

Got up to go to the can in the middle of the night. Damn prostate. I thought I heard someone clear their throat. Just getting off of a double, hallucination was a common side effect of sleep deprivation. I saw my son's Rottweiler sitting in front of the stove.

'Pardon me, do you have any Grey Poupon? I must have some for this sandwich.'

Being a doctor, you have a clear sense of what is possible in the world and what isn't, so I shook my head and went on to the bathroom. When I finished I came out to find the dog blocking the doorway.

'Perhaps you didn't hear me.'

'No, no, I heard you. I simply don't believe you're talking, so I am going back to bed to get some sleep.'

'You're not even curious how I came by this roast beef sandwich?'

'Roast Beef?' Stomach rumbled. 'Okay, I'll bite. Where did you get the sandwich?'

'I feel so guilty telling you. Okay, you twisted my tail. The twins gave it to me. I was supposed to keep quiet while they went to the concert.'

'The Metalhead concert? The one they were forbidden to attend?'

'Not my job. I just wanted some mustard. I knew you would take care of me if I just asked.'

'So when are they getting back?'

'Uh, I can talk, but I still can't tell time.'

'Fine, let's split that sandwich and wait. I'll get the mustard.'

'Did I mention that aromatic herb I've seen them smoking out back?'

'No, tell me more.'

And so he did. I discovered things about my sons, I wasn't sure I wanted to know. As I closed up the mustard jar, the Rottweiler remarked, 'Those thumbs are truly amazing. I heard you were a surgeon. Any chance I could have some thumbs?'

'As a matter of fact, I have two sons who won't be using theirs after tonight. You have four paws and they have four thumbs. Can you wash dishes?'

'Sorry, my resume includes biting, barking, ear-hustling, crotch-sniffing and talking to you. Dishwashing not included.'

'Just as well, they are going to need those thumbs for all the chores they will be doing.'

'They're coming.'

'I don't hear anything.'

He cocks his head and rotates his ears. 'Dog, remember?'

I turned off the light in the kitchen and waited. They would have to pass me to get to their room. I could smell the concert all over them; the beer, marijuana and cigarettes. Ugh.

'Evening, boys. Say hello to your new warden.'

The dog barks at them, a series of sharp, staccato sounds.

Looking at the boys, 'He says you are going to like it here at our new facility. Go to your rooms and take a shower. Lawn mowing at 8:00 AM. Sharp.' I smiled at the dog, 'Adding to your resume already...'

Shoe Fly Baby

L.A. Craig

Shoo Fly, Don't Bother Me. Never understood that song. How do you belong to somebody, never mind feel like a morning star?

He sent a birthday card of a shoe. I sniffed his signature. It smelled of white nothing. A kiss underneath. I tucked it in the corner of the mirror.

He kissed me outside the labs once, long and deep. We got whistled, but didn't care. Hours later in life class, my insides still shimmered with the aftershock and my fingers twitched to sketch his face.

Call me, he'd written at the bottom of the card. Yeah right.

In my mind Oceanography implied an ethical conscience, principled students, morally incapable of being three-timing rats. His geochemistry lecturer, some bitch he met at a tidal flats weekend, and yours truly. I was all art-student-brash to his check-shirted nerd, but the contrast was the attraction. His sweet temper. Docile compared to my impulsive urges. I thought he smoothed my corners. Never dreamt he'd possess an inner caveman.

A lime green slip-on with purple trim, cerise background. The shades not strictly true to Warhol's Shoe Fly Baby, but I still love it. The block colours, black outline, take no nonsense. I'm a shoe. Deal with it. Yet the image is a cartoon; a joke. I should rip it to tiny shreds. He won't have picked it for any artistic merit. I can see him now, shoe... doh, Emmie likes shoes. Isn't that how dick-thinkers operate? Maybe I should send a thank-you-for-the-card card with a picture of the sea.

Today, a week later, he rings.

'It's me, Em.'

I want to say get lost, leave me in peace you waste of my time, but there's a wink from the mirror.

'Get my card?'

'I did.'

'It just jumped into my hand. Had you all over it.' He waited.

Quiet.

'Em, I…'

'It's in the bin,' I spit. Trash. Like you thought me, I almost say, but the words won't come.

More silence while my brain tries to get this right.

'Let me fix it, Em.'

I've missed his voice. Like a tranquilliser, it numbs me from his deceit, tugs at my soft bits and ties that addictive knot my gut craves. In my head, I'm in his arms.

Now I smell him.

I pluck the card from the mirror. The colours begin to needle, too intense; a pimped-up version of the original.

'We're right together Emmie.'

He's an utter twat, but the stupid in me still wants it to be true.

I lift my foot, place the copy of Warhol's masterpiece next to my size six.

Cinderella didn't fake the fit.

Life Drawing

Ariel Dawn

Not naked, he says, nude. Not you, womanhood. He gives directions, and his grey eyes drive my body to the most aesthetically pleasing position: left hip and elbow on the paint-stained rug, sky-lit.

This happens in an alley. Outside the window is another window, and a room behind wicker baskets: sun shadows play inside. I wait for someone to open a door and see I'm naked as a child or an animal. My posture is hollow. My lover didn't want my love.

He snaps his fingers to draw my mind back to the rug, the aching hip bone and sleeping leg. He reveals the drawing. No line between skin and air, a charcoal blur, the woman barely formed, half-there.

He offers it to me, though when I ask for his signature, he laughs and closes the door.

Omelettes

R. A. Martens

The stranger came limping over the hill from the north one evening while we were at our meal. He carried pipes under one arm, and under the other, a creature we had never seen before. We gave him hospitality, and when he had eaten and drunk, we asked him what the beast was.

'This is a city,' he said. Seeing the looks on our faces he added: 'It may seem unassuming whilst it sleeps, but don't be taken in.' He asked for more drink, and said that he would play his pipes for us. The sound was not to our taste. Indeed, we have killed travellers for less, since, but we were mild folk back then. The city snored fitfully at the traveller's feet, and didn't stir for the whole of the tune. We made sure the man had a drink in both hands for the rest of the night, and when his head fell back, one of us took the pipes and threw them in the lake.

In the morning, the man was too concerned with keeping his head and his stomach attached to his body to notice the pipes were missing. He mentioned them two days later, but did not seem upset when they couldn't be found. We suspected they were stolen, and the city, perhaps, was stolen too. It walked slowly around the village on its thick stone legs as though looking for the way home, and its chimneys huffed with outrage if anyone stared for too long. 'Doesn't like to be looked at,' said the man. He never smiled when he looked at the city, but I couldn't quite call his expression fear, either.

One morning when we were still in our beds, we heard a protracted and violent argument, and when we rose, the traveller was by the fire, breaking eggs as big as a fist into the pan. He had a gouge out of his arm where the city had taken exception, but whistled contentedly to himself as he cooked. I have never before or since tasted anything so good as a city-egg. We were disappointed to learn that it laid only once a month. Where had the city come from? we asked the traveller. Was there a place where they roamed the hills in packs? What did they eat? What did the young look like? He shook his head. This was the only city he had ever seen, and he knew no more about it than we did.

We have learned to leave a bowl of beer for the city at nights, so that if it lays in the morning it is too drowsy to attack us when we take its eggs. People come for miles to taste our omelettes. The stranger is dead.

Planets

Vanessa Gebbie

That last day, when we woke, I had a little door in my heart and so did you. You put your ear close to mine, and I to yours. It felt good, like that.

You laughed. 'I hear the scream of gulls, I feel the pull of the moon.'

I could not tell you what I heard, or felt. It was not good, so I made it up. 'A volcano. The stink of fish n chips.'

'No,' you said. 'Honest... wait...' and you got up on one elbow, peered deep, squinting. 'It is a cool, clear October morning in your heart. The sea, no, not the sea... hundreds of helical waveguides. Can't you feel them?'

Maybe I didn't believe you. Maybe I didn't want to believe you. I smelled your hair, just there, could see each strand so clearly, as if lit by a sudden ray of light. Your scalp. The scent of wood pulp, the pillow, lavender...

Something was lightening, becoming clear, as when a long forgetfulness lifts. I started to speak. 'Listen...'

You hushed me. 'Don't speak. When you speak I can see the walls of your heart, moving, veined. Your resting heart beat rises...'

'But...'

You smiled. 'No. Don't speak. I keep waking at 4 am, trying to remember something — done it for days, now I know...'

So I didn't. Speak. Maybe I should have.

You coughed. Shifted position. 'A whole system, honest. I see a whole system, in your heart. Like...' you peered again. 'You won't believe this...'

I was believing it. But I never said. Just wondered how to tell you what I saw.

You prattled on like a small boy. 'Two earth-sized planets.

Blue, white, just like...'

I think that's when I decided you had to go. I mean, who would...

And in the kitchen, after I told you, you turned away. Held on to the surface near the sink, gazed out of the window. At the roofs opposite. The sky, maybe.

My chest hurt. Like there was something going on in there. Like planets were colliding.

How

Calum Kerr

I don't know how to do this.

The black plastic of the bag in my hand is slippery with sweat. I'm aware that my fingers are rubbing over the slick surface again and again, but I don't know how to stop. I am unable to cross the threshold. I can't make myself take the extra step.

It's been weeks since I went into his room. I can't speak for Sally. I don't know what she does when I'm at work, or shopping, or drinking. She barely leaves the house now. I doubt I could avoid coming in here if I was her.

I think she comes in here some nights. She leaves the bed while I stare at the ceiling. I hear her moving around the house. Maybe she comes in here to sit and remember.

And now this: this instruction, this edict.

She wants the room cleared. She wants to move on. She doesn't want to remember anymore.

But I don't know how to do this.

Shadows

Emma Shaw

I was outside, looking in; they were inside but not looking out. I was wreathed in shadows; they were bathed in the harsh light of the fluorescents which seemed only the more to illuminate their loneliness. I was concealed; they were in a fishbowl but didn't seem to notice or perhaps just didn't care.

The young blond server cleans, the cherrywood counter gleams. Polished coffee urns reflect the light, distorting the faces of the diner's occupants. The red-headed dame concentrates on something in her hand, a sandwich maybe, but she isn't eating. Perhaps she's just checking her nails? She ignores the coffee in front of her, and the man beside her. They are together but continents apart. No one speaks, no one smiles.

But the other man, the single man sitting hunched over, is the one that interests me. If I could read his thoughts I might go into the diner. He may be my salvation, but just as likely he is my nemesis. I have watched him every night for weeks, hoping to have some sign that his reason for being there is me and that he can relieve me of the dark burden I carry. But he just sits, stares, stirs his coffee. Doesn't look round at the street outside, the shop opposite, the darkened windows above. Just sits, as if he expects me to walk in and say, 'Hi. I'm the guy you're looking for. I'm the killer but, see, it wasn't my fault.'

If he is the man from the FBI then I have a chance to tell my story and get justice. If he is the man from the Giacometti Family then I'm dead before I open my mouth. He should wear big letters on the back of his suit, so that I know.

Do I take the risk and go in or carry on skulking in the shadows, living what has become my half-life? Would it be so bad to have my head blown off? At least then it would be over.

Or, worst case scenario, what if he is Mr FBI and also Giacometti's button man?

And, again, maybe I am mistaken and he's just another lonely night-hawk whiling away the hours until dawn.

Each night I consider the options but I guess I'm still a coward and I shrink back into the shadows to resume my own life of solitude and paranoia.

Second Look: Goat With Lawnmower

Claire Collison

It was in the gallery with the terrible acoustics the goat seduced me. The echoing white gallery, purpose-built, set above the public *fuente*, where washerwomen used to wash their dirty clothes. Unsympathetic to the scale of skinny side streets, where caged birds made a din. The one-woman show was works on silk: kit paints in sweetie colours, mounted badly and eccentrically hung on lengths of cane (she'd fussed about them being touched, the curator confided).

Considering the astrological content, I liked them more than I'd expected: they were touching, naive, brut. But the one that got me was the goat: on hind legs, its front hooves propping a lawnmower, the way a mother would push a pram. Even as I write this now I wish I'd bought it. In the foreground were flowers; across the top ran the legend: Virgo; a constellation, and the dates: 21st to 21st. The curator said the artist had once been Dali's muse (though she pronouced it 'moose'). I said, 'I'm guessing: hippy, seventies' - could almost smell joss sticks; hear the shuffle of tarot cards. ('Yes,' the curator said; 'She's got a set.') Had I not met her, I'd have liked her paintings better.

Over the following week the goat niggled like a photograph not taken. I got a pang as I swam - a dread he'd been sold. I telephoned, agonising as the curator wondered – tried (echoingly) to remember...

'No, not the goat,' she said, with no urgency.

'I'm coming now, with the cash.'

'You'll meet the artist, then.'

'Don't mention anything yet; I still might decide not to buy. But I need a second look.'

She was all white in pedalpushers; her hair once-flame now not; crisp cotton shirt, rope espadrilles, support bandage around her right ankle. She leant on the marble balustrade above the *fuente*, like a Rivera girl remembering her plait. A parrot in a too-small cage whistled. We spoke in Castilian, native tongue of neither one of us. She saw no irony in giving a goat a lawnmower – certainly didn't thank me for suggesting it - had simply represented the 'industriousness and masculinity' of all those born in late August. (I remembered a goatherd; his goats pouring like rain down the mountain, the mournful clanging of their bells.) I tried smaller talk: how long ago had she painted it? At first I thought she must have misunderstood; so flustered, so defensive, so not 'a year ago. Or possibly two. Can't remember exactly. Does it matter?' No, I assured her. But it did: she'd lied – and knew that I knew she had. And I couldn't live with it all on my wall: it was too burdensome. Not naive at all.

Below us, I watched as modern families parked up four by fours, filling their plastic bottles from the *fuente*. The gushing sound they made was a second or so out of sync, swilling through the echoing white gallery.

http://www.medicaldictionary-forthewoundedheart.com/gonorrhoea

Ian Shine

What is gonorrhoea?

Gonorrhoea (from the Latin *gonos* 'seed' and *rhoe* 'flow') is a sexually transmitted disease, making it one of the few diseases that can be contracted in an enjoyable manner.

What causes gonorrhoea?

The bacteria *Neisseria gonorrhoeae*, which reside in warm, moist body cavities, namely the kind most likely to be licked, flicked and dipped into by the young salmon that is the sexually aroused tongue. In our case study (*see below*), this tongue erratically and occasionally erotically jumped from place to place, burying itself in sweet and sweated kernels of salted female flesh, insatiable in its desire to dig out *Neisseria*, which, to the untrained ear, might sound like the name of the local girl one would find in a story about a foreigner falling briefly in love in a small Greek village. The protagonist might like the look of *Neisseria* after half a bottle of ouzo, but he'd rather not take her home and have her to hold, from this day forth; for better, for worse; til death them do part.

What are the symptoms of gonorrhoea?

Symptoms are numerous and will be understood differently depending upon an individual's circumstances. A man contracting gonorrhoea from the wife he thought monogamous may wish to immediately rinse away these reminders of infidelity. However, our case study — a boy/man devirginised on his 18th birthday by a girl/woman whom he was convinced he would marry, but who was delivered to the grave that same evening by a bus passing outside the boy/man's house — instead wishes to harbour these symptoms and tenderly dab them every day:

- **Red or swollen opening of the penis**
For our case study, this will represent the rose, the flower of love, cracking into bud on the once bold stem. It may bloom particularly furiously during urination (*see below*), dyeing itself deep crimson like a child embarrassed before a medical professional. It may also be worn like a poppy, for every day is now Remembrance Day.

- **Burning during urination**
There is nothing worse, or more common for the bereaved, than absence of sensation. For this reason, our case study may wish to hold tight to this liquid tug which runs a sizzling slither along his rod (*see Hemingway-Santiago syndrome*).

- **Discharge from the penis (white, yellow and/or green)**
A rainbow is the last reminder of a sunny day once the rain arrives. Ergo, this gonorrhoea sufferer's husbandry of his technicolour discharge will be a surrogate for the uxoriousness he never got to cultivate.

- **Tender or swollen testicles**
Coleridge spoke of the albatross around his mariner's neck, and so we all have our burdens to bear, reminding us of the things we have done:

> But rail not against the balls between thy legs,
> Though they may cause you pain;
> For if again you had the chance to dance that dance,
> You'd do it all again.

What is the best treatment for gonorrhoea?
In this case, none. Treatment may do more emotional harm than learning to live with the disease.

Takeaway Poetry Joint

Thomas McColl

Hello sir. Thank you for calling the Takeaway Poetry Joint. Before we go any further, I would just like to inform you that today's special offer is one free bottle of drink and portion of garlic bread with any large poem, plus free delivery by a performance poet... I know, sounds good, doesn't it? Do you have our menu there in front of you?... Good... Yes, it's a long list, isn't it? The 'Full English' we like to call it — everything from Alvarez to Zephaniah...which, when you think about it, takes you both from A to Z and from A to B — if you get my drift... Yes sir, you're in a rush, I understand... Yes, I can certainly make a suggestion... Perhaps you'd like to choose Ted Hughes, deep pan?... With this one there's a choice of four different toppings: There's 'Pike', part of our 'sag belly' promotion (two for the price of one), or 'Thistles' (though we only suggest you try this if you have a rubber tongue), or 'Crow', a cheesy myth (albeit well-done), or, finally, 'The Jaguar', with which we're offering a pass for two to see the real thing (be completely unaware it's in a cage) at the local zoo... No, none of these suit you?... Oh, you'd prefer something lighter... How about Michael Rosen, thin and crispy?... With that we have the 'Don't Put Mustard in the Custard' topping... Yes, this one has both mustard and custard, sir... I know: They say don't, but we do... That's what we're like at the Takeaway Poetry Joint... You'd like that one?... Great! No probs. A brave but excellent choice, sir... And the poet who's doing the delivery is Thomas McColl... Yes, if he's longer than fifteen minutes you get your money back — but trust me, sir, with this particular dish, he should be no more than a minute or two...

In Which a Man is Washing his Hands

Sarah Hilary

The lake is a glass half-full of mountains, topped with a froth of clouded sky. A red sailboat hangs at the lip of the lake, its shadow showing in sharp relief the corrugations of the brushwork.

Everything about the painting screams, 'Old.'

Its frame is the colour of cinnamon, the wood acned by worm, or more likely by a steel toothpick, one of the tools of the faker's trade.

You dislike the painting on sight, and on principle. It's trying too hard and you've been taught that's how to spot a forgery: 'The varnish will be too cracked, or the frame too distressed. Some old frauds stick cobwebs between the stretchers at the back.'

Originals don't scream. They whisper.

A strand of red tickles your cheek and you take a moment to twist it back with the rest of your hair, pinning it out of the way. Pinching at the latex gloves, you finish your fingertip examination of the canvas. Minutely, because there is something here, you can hear it, something more than a fraud. Your fingers coax the something closer to its skin, but you need the camera. You need to X-ray its bones.

Cameras never lie; beneath the glassy lake you spy not a skeleton but a ghost.

The phantom of another painting.

'Rare,' it whispers. 'Priceless.'

You see –

The washing of a man's hands in a room of statues.

Vermeer, drowning under a lake of clouds.

# #

Stephen McGeagh

I am Katy Perry's biggest fan and I hope that one day she will tweet me back because she is always on twitter and so am I. I spend a long time waiting for new tweets to pop up on my feed. I think that I should follow more people than 219 people because then I will get more new tweets more often. I don't follow any more than 219 people though, because 219 is too many really. Some of them don't say anything. They are silent. They are real people and they are boring in real life. They don't understand twitter so they don't tweet. If they do tweet it comes out wrong. Like a status update. That is not the point.

News moves fast on twitter. People are exposed and they send pictures of their breasts to their 10m followers by mistake, when they are releasing new albums. People are heroic charity Jesus shining bastards and then public masturbaters in the same week. People lose their minds and tweet-feud. Footballers quote Morissey and give out horse-racing tips. Katy Perry is lovely to everyone. She re-tweets her fans. She makes everyone feel like they are her BFF. I am too scared to tweet Katy Perry because I am afraid that she won't tweet me back or re-tweet my tweet and then I will either kill myself or I won't go on twitter for a while.

I join pinterest and I stay on facebook and I try to blog and I use google images to find tattoo designs and I read wikipedia pages, on my smartphone, about the Armenian genocide while I'm in the pub, drinking alone. I plug in my headphones and I start up a youtube play list of late 90s nu-metal and this helps me to do all the things that I am trying to achieve that day.

I would like to stand in a field. The air would be cold and the sun would be going down behind a big tree at one end of the field. The grass would be long and I would be wearing denim shorts and the grass would tickle my knees. I would have a vest on and my arms would be like the arms of a guy who cuts down trees for a living. I would be stood behind Katy Perry and she would be watching the sunset. She would be thinking this sunset is incredible, I will remember it for the rest of my life. She would feel like crying with happiness because she had been given a few seconds of her own to watch a sunset over a cold, long-grass field. I would reach out to touch her on the shoulder and then stop myself. Then she would walk off slowly and go back to her stressful job and her stressful life and I would stay in the cold dark field for rest of my life because I would never be that close to Katy Perry again.

The Woman in the Bowl

Danielle McLaughlin

The antique shop was hot, airless, badly lit. She had stepped inside to escape the rain, pretending to examine a porcelain chamber pot. She hoped the shower would pass quickly – Jeremy didn't like supper to be late. Looking around, she saw boxes of china, prints in cheap frames, a rail of moth-bitten fur coats. Beneath the coats, on a wooden table, were three mink stoles. The stoles lay balding and jaded, so inviting in their glassy-eyed surrender that she wanted to climb onto the table, lay herself down beside them.

On a shelf, set apart from the general clutter, was a bowl in a blue and white pattern. She ran a finger through the dust and saw a woman wearing a kimono. The woman's lips were parted, as if she had cried out when the glaze was being poured. There were trees also, and some birds and a bridge.

'Early nineteenth century. Mind you don't go putting it in the dish-washer.'

She jumped as an elderly man emerged from the back of the shop. 'I don't have a dish-washer. Jeremy doesn't like them.'

'I was joking,' he said. 'That's a Thomas Minton, circa 1820. Purely ornamental, of course. You can see it's finished with a lead glaze.'

She looked again at the bowl and thought she saw the woman's mouth twitch. 'How much is it?'

The price almost caused her to drop the bowl, but she had put aside a little money over the years, money Jeremy didn't know about.

Jeremy slurped as he ate, scraped his spoon against the bottom of the bowl. She flinched, imagining metal drawn across the woman's delicate face. The soup was tomato - blood red and acidic. The best, according to the book she had consulted in the library. Or rather, the worst. Later, she rinsed out the bowl and held it up to the light. She touched the fine cracks that lined the woman's forehead, wondered when they would grow deeper.

The deterioration was gradual, subtle - a kind she understood. When he tired of soup, she tried pork in a sharp soy sauce, vegetables pickled in vinegar. She knew how to wait. The evening she discovered him slumped over the table, his pulse weak, his breathing ragged, she did not run to the telephone in the hall. Instead, she took the bowl to the sink, washed it, patted it dry. She traced with her finger what little remained of the blue and white pattern. The woman in the bowl had gone. She imagined her laughing, running through trees that no longer existed, leaving behind, on the rim of the bowl, a fragment of blue and white kimono.

Celery

Jim O'Loughlin

Before you take a bite, pause for a moment and tell yourself you are in an Edith Wharton novel. It is late 19th century New York and you are attending a midwinter dinner party. As an invited guest, you are appropriately attired in evening wear and looking forward to decadent dinner featuring terrapin soup, scalloped oysters with cream, broiled duck, and peach-fed ham. It looks delicious, but it all seems so heavy, and you have been suffering from indigestion. You desire nothing more than a crisp apple right now, but they are out of season and you know not to expect for quite some time.

But then your attention is drawn to a glass vase in the center of the dinner table. The vase is filled with tall, stalky stems with green leaves at the top. It is an odd looking bouquet, particularly for such a formal event. Your hostess, who looks surprisingly like Edith Wharton, must sense your confusion, because she approaches and informs you that the vase contains not flowers, but celery, sent all the way from California on one of those new refrigerated rail cars. Can you imagine such a thing?

Your hostess, let's call her Edith, reaches into the vase and pulls out a stem. Then she brings it up to her mouth and takes a loud bite. You could not be more surprised if she had started chewing on a rose bush.

Of course, you have had celery before, as part of a sauce with fowl. But uncooked like this? It hardly seems civilized. Yet, it would be rude to demure when Edith gestures to the vase, so you pick up a stem and take a nibble. It is crunchy, not wholly unlike an apple, and it seems that it has been months since you have eaten anything that was not boiled to mush.

You take a full bite and chew with gusto, ignoring the celery string that has gotten caught in your teeth. Edith smiles a knowing smile and hands you a napkin, and you suspect she knows more about you than you know about yourself.

And now when you eat celery, a vegetable that is available by the bagful in the market at any time of year, you tell yourself to be this character in an Edith Wharton novel, to imagine celery as a rare, hard food in a world of boiled meats. Approach each bite as a delicacy, an impossible taste of summer in a long, cold winter

Perfectly Black Sky

Amanda Oosthuizen

'Have you ever had a recurring nightmare?' Larry asks. We drive golf balls once a month; tonight, for the first time, he's invited me to his studio.

'Not since college. But we all had nightmares, drilling into a nasal passage mostly.'

'Did it ever happen to you?' He turns to face me. His eyes are deep brown and single-minded. I'd always assumed his life was as muddled and confusing as mine.

'It happens to everyone in my line of work.'

'My nightmare concerns the most important job of my life. The 'Rite of Spring' for the Mariinsky at the Théâtre des Champs-Élysées. A massive solo starts the whole ballet.'

'Every bassoonist's dream, I suppose.'

'Stravinsky wanted it to sound as if one is 'striving for the unattainable'. In my nightmare, I'm on the Metro and the train doesn't stop. I eventually catch a taxi, the traffic's jammed. I jump out, run and discover I've left my bassoon in the boot.'

I chuckle but he's grim-faced.

'At the theatre, I check my jacket for the reed case. It's not there. I borrow a reed. Of course it's no good. As I'm warming up, the rollers drop off the instrument. I never actually get to play.'

'It's just a nightmare, Larry.'

'The point is I've got the job. I'm standing in for the Mariinsky principal on Saturday.' His fingers twitch. 'At the Champs-Élysées.'

A silence forms between us. Larry's frowning over his reeds, cutting little pieces of wire.

'Will you play it to me?' I ask.

He takes a reed from a small black case, props it in water and lifts a bassoon from the rack. Slipping a strap over his head, he plugs in a silver crook and slots on the reed.

He breathes as if filling the deepest well. His jaw drops and, with his chest taut, he sounds the first note. I understand Stravinsky's intention, his 'striving for the unattainable' because it's a note that holds the entire universe.

They say if you dream of teeth, you're suffering from stress. That night, I dream of teeth on the Paris Metro and the London Underground, teeth in every state of decay. I wake knowing my solos have lacked richness and buy a ticket for the ballet.

Saturday, I catch the Eurostar from St Pancras to the Gare du Nord.

The theatre is a bold art deco building. Inside, marble covers every surface. The musicians take their places. A weight lifts from my chest when I spot Larry already seated at the back of the pit, but I remember what's coming. The lights dim. Valery Gergiev takes a bow. I watch Larry place his reed on the instrument and inhale. His sound streams from the pit like lava defying gravity.

After the show, I wait outside the theatre but I don't see Larry. I hope he's gone for a celebratory drink. It's a perfectly black sky. I walk through the night towards the brightest lights.

Her 12 Faces

Dan Powell

12.
The wide-grin of the young woman you no longer are, behind which sits the shadow of all the years since we last spoke. In my head you're still twenty.

11.
The face I attempt to extrapolate, to engineer from the ever youthful one in my head. Adding years and cares and lines and density, I try to make you my contemporary again. I fail.

10.
Nervous blinking eyes and trembling lips that told me, months after we had last spoken, of the baby that might have been, that never was. It was my turn for creased disappointment, my face that folded like arms.

9.
The tender lust, lips and eyes brimming with it, that, months after our latest break-up, I followed back to your bed thinking it was for me, until you spoke someone else's name.

8.
The hope illuminating every pore of you at graduation, that shone bright as we tried again, that guttered as we left in separate cars that drove down separate motorways.

7.
Your eyes exploding suns each time I left to meet the girl who came after you. The pair of us waiting for the end of university, for when we might truly and finally part.

6.

The second time you dumped me? The third? I lost count somewhere. This time just tiredness weighing on the edges of your eyes, pulling at the corners of your mouth. Tiredness, and relief when I agree.

5.

Your face blurred with tears, your voice raw with cries. The night I brought someone else back to the house we shared with friends. You didn't want me but your didn't want anyone else to have me and so we collapsed back into each other.

4.

The coldness that swept out from your brow the first time you dumped me. The sheerness of you expression providing no handhold or foothold with which to ascend. In the pokey room we shared that summer you seemed unreachable.

3.

Disappointment creasing your face, folding your features like arms when I came clean about seeing your housemate behind your back. It was only two nights. We never shagged. But you never quite came back after that.

2.

Close-up, eyes wide, lips parting. That moment before our first kiss. So close I can see the nightclub's disco lights reflected in your eyes.

1.

Coming from Stoke Road, I emerge from the subway back into the autumn sun of 1992 to see you crossing the circle of grass at the centre of the pedestrianised roundabout. If I'd happened along more than a minute earlier I'd have had my back to you as you arrived, would not have seen your primrose patterned summer dress and the wide grin that broke across your face like a dawning sun as we first laid eyes upon each other.

Vigil (After Bruno Schulz)
John Keating

Every day, that whole summer, there passed not a word between us. My father would read for hours, scratching his head, and I would watch him. Then he would get up and walk to his desk, unroll a large sheet of paper and take a pen from behind his ear. Hours of writing while I watched him. Then he would turn to me and I would read and then shake my head.

We went on long journeys out to the countryside to relax and enjoy ourselves. But from black tunnels to red bricks and then green, we kept on losing our fellow passengers to the broken doors. You could see them as they flew past the window, trying to tell us something.

When I slept, he would watch me sleeping and the sweat drying on my forehead as I concentrated on the dream. A dead raven, with its beak open, and a wet panoptic eye.

Rose Petal Eyes

Tracey Upchurch

The teacher told us in a hushed voice, 'Mary's mum has passed away.' Like she was food. .. passed around, passed away. The teacher paused, looking around at us, glancing into our eyes to check for sadness before flicking away again. We weren't upset, though; Mary was nice but none of us knew her mum – she'd been ill for ages so Mary never had us home for tea.

'Poor Mary,' we said, trying to care but not managing to, not at school. School wasn't the place for that; caring was done at home.

Caring happened on my pillow that night. I heard Mum clattering about with the dishes, down in the kitchen, and I imagined her dead. Pictured her deep in the earth, cold and away, and me coming home from school to a giant hole, a nothing. No chat. Who'd make tea? No hug. Every day?

I imagined it until it felt nearly real and my eyes streamed and snot clogged up my nose. I choked and heard her pause, as if she'd heard me imagining her dead, then I felt stupid so I wiped my face with my sleeve and left Mary to cry her own way to rose petal eyes – because, thank God, it was her mum dead not mine.

Mary got on the school bus the next day. She looked normal but blank, as if she were looking at her own insides. I wanted to give her a hug but this was the school bus, so I hurried to sit next to someone else instead. We all did.

Once we were a safe distance from Mary's mum's death, we all turned around to stare.

Reasons to be Cheerful Part 4

Holly Howitt

Mum always said it's easier to be miserable than cheerful. She said she was onto something, dear old mum, and that I had to learn. She said she'd teach me the ways of the world, the fucking sorry ways. She'd sit with a fag in the corner of her thin, stripped mouth and even when I was a kid the lines were so clear around her lips it was like her whole face had been torn apart and sewn back together by a madman. Anyway, with fag ash falling into that chipped floral saucer, she'd remind me that finding reasons to be cheerful was a bloody chore, nodding somewhat sagely with her hair rollers bouncing in agreement. Dear old mum.

I'm sitting mimicking dear old mum, but instead of a chipped tea plate, I've got a takeaway coffee cup for my fag ash. I've got into this routine of sitting on this stoop outside the coffee shop and having a first morning fag with my latte. It makes me feel a bit French, even though I'm currently in Essex. Reasons to be cheerful. Ok, that can be number one. A hot coffee on a cool day, and a fag for dessert. Clouds rolling to reveal a bright blue beach-new day. Yep. That's number two. And number three? Well, I'm pretty sure the barista just winked at me, hands covered in foam and all smirky. A nice wink though – not too pervy but not too polite. And my big old number four. Number four is that dear old mum's dead. She wasn't onto anything: it's not hard to find reasons to be cheerful at all. Dear old mum. It's just an anagram for Ma Doledrum.

Broom

Natalie Bowers

Silvia opens the door to the under-stairs cupboard. It's dark inside, but she doesn't need to be able to see to find what she's looking for.

'Top quality broom this,' Joe had said as he'd leant it against the back wall, between the fuse box and the shelf of spare light bulbs. 'It'll last.'

Silvia reaches into the cupboard. Joe had been right; for 42 years it had swept away the debris of their lives.

'Oh, your beautiful hair! What have you done? Give me those scissors!'

'That bloody cat! If I have to chase one more pigeon around this house ...'

'Don't you walk away from me! Don't you dare slam that ...'

'Oh, Joe, they're lovely. The petals have just about dropped off the last bunch.'

Silvia's fingers find what they're looking for. The paint has flaked away, but the wood is smooth and warm, like a child's skin.

'Mum! Mum! We need a mast for our pirate ship.'

'We need a gun for our tank.'

'Our fort needs a flagpole.'

As she lifts the broom over the mushroom of carrier bags, she tries to straighten her back, but it's as arched as the handle. If she had the strength she'd string it like an archer's bow and lead her grandchildren in a game of Cowboys and Indians.

Silvia feels a gentle hand on her shoulder.

'They'll have their own brooms there, Mum.'

'I know, love,' she says and turns away from the cupboard, toward the open front door.

Changing Light

Amanda Quinn

On my first visit I noticed a copy of *The Great Gatsby*. I concentrated on the details of the cover; Farrow and Redford in a hazy sunlit embrace, the title picked out in 1980s wine bar art deco. Very cool, I thought, to have chosen that particular edition.

It made me overlook things. Like James Gatz looking up at the deck of that drunken savage's yacht and seeing nothing but gleaming wood and brass.

He wasn't my Gatsby. Or my Daisy. He was a cold and brutish Tom Buchanan with the drab, murderous heart of George Wilson. The book wasn't even his. It had been left in his flat by 'some pretentious student girl'.

I re-read my own copy afterwards. Funny how the book had changed since my own breathless youth. Now it seemed a mean tale about a crook and a spoilt girl. I didn't believe in the green light anymore. Or perhaps I couldn't see it from where I was standing.

You're About To Find Out Who I Am

Amy Mackelden

You tell me I'm text book, that if we fucked you'd start analysis immediately, calculate my BMI, log it next to my shoe size and what I give Spielberg movies out of ten. Always a six or a seven.

I say, 'Analyse away. I'll fill a form out if it gets you.' You find a ruler and measure the distance between our mouths, ask, 'How is two centimetres and how about four?' But I'd prefer to be a negative equation, without a plastic end point. You've had dinner with all the men that we work with and have seen every Reese Witherspoon movie, even the serious ones I didn't think anyone saw. You're a completist; I want you in spite of this.

Before you leave, one hand in your bag trying to locate missed calls, I hold the ruler for you. 'This is too far,' I tell you. On the porch you ask, 'And now?' But this is not one of those girl-getting shows where season one builds to a crescendo kiss. This is a police procedural in which criminals eat people. And soon, we're bones.

Autumn

John Paul O'Neill

Alex feels like he has been alive an awful long time today, slouched in contemplation on a green park bench, trying indecisively to banish away the damnable autumn blues. An awful long time, as long as the Thames lapping weakly to the pulse of a pallid veil of sunlight.

If people weren't busy convincing themselves that love really does exist they'd be jumping off every available bridge and promontory of the London skyline. Lack of sex is one thing, the frustration might sicken, momentarily unhinged, but there is relief for that.

High up from a plain tree a leaf floats off, lumbering onto Alex's head and then onto the pavement.

'Bloody autumn!' he mutters.

Lack of sex is one thing, lack of love is a much more serious proposition. He tries to identify part of his torso, patting his quilted coat. It hurts, actually hurts, just there, well everywhere, lack of love isn't a localised pain, it creeps in everywhere when you least expect it. That heartache that you thought you left behind is back, playing havoc with every mental and physical process.

A city with millions of people, loving most everything. If people weren't busy convincing themselves that love really does exist they'd be putting on a show, jumping off every available bridge, promontory and South Bank park bench.

Orange

Sonya Oldwin

The trip was his idea — a long weekend away in Devon. Not that he said so, but I'm taking it as his way of apologising for the other night. And before we got on the road, I thought this was what we needed. Time alone with one another, long walks along the seafront, a cottage with a fire place.

But.

We've been stuck in traffic for two hours and we're not even out of London. The M25 is a nightmare. I'm hungry. I'm thirsty. I take an orange out of my bag and leave the pen knife in there. I don't think we should have sharp, pointy objects on display right now. I take the peel off in tiny pieces, careful not to tear into the fruit.

'Do you have to eat that?'

'I'm starving. Thought we'd be near a Little Chef by now.'

He pinches his nose, rubs his eyes. He claims he's allergic to citrus fruit. It's bollocks. He forgets I know, he told me all about it after his fifth Mojito one night. He cannot stand the smell, that's all.

'Not my fault, is it? We should be half-way to Torquay.'

Not his fault. No, it never is. It wasn't his fault that he cheated on me, he would have been helpless against two girls, after all. I only caught him because I wasn't supposed to be in town that night. I'd lost my voice, I couldn't go on stage. So, in effect, I'm to blame that we're stuck in road trip hell. Punishment for being ill at an inopportune moment. I wonder how many girls force themselves on him when I'm touring.

'Turn around.'

'You think the thought hasn't occurred to me? Other direction is just as bad.'

'That's not what I mean. We're going back. I'm getting my things out of your place. We're done.'

Never mind the infidelity, I can't be with a man who fakes an allergic reaction every time I peel an orange. How peculiar that I've only just realised this.

Annie

Emma J. Lannie

Annie isn't okay. She isn't okay in any sense of the word. From under the table, she watches the feet. Shoes with scuff marks on the toes. Shoes with laces loose, unravelling, undoing themselves. No one can see her here. From her below-knee vantage point, she is unknown to the room's occupants. She fights her breathing, slows the fast, makes it quiet.

They are talking in whispers. If she could see their lips, she might be able to guess at the words. The carpet, she notices, has a stain the shape of Italy, right by her left knee. She doesn't know how long she will have to stay here. She is not okay. Annie closes her eyes.

Annie wonders if she should have done things differently. If she would have, if she'd known this was where she would end up. And now there is no undoing it. It's done, and she is underneath the table staring at a stain and glimpsing out to watch two pairs of feet pace the room.

She was supposed to leave twenty minutes ago.

They are still in the room. One of the feet taps without any discernible rhythm. Annie isn't okay. She didn't expect she'd be trapped here like this. She thought they'd have given up and gone away when she didn't answer the door. Instead, she watched in horror as the handle turned. Diving under the table was instinct. Annie now realises this may have been a mistake.

Two legs hover right next to the table. Annie holds her breath, but her heart's crescendo fills her ears. She worries that she is not okay, that she will have a heart attack and collapse and then be found. And then how will she explain it, her being under the table this whole time?

Annie didn't honestly think he would turn up. They hadn't made definite plans. She'd been being polite. Perhaps, she thinks, she'd smiled at the wrong thing, at a part when her smiling could be taken to be consensus, a yes. Right now, Annie should be open-mouthed, with her dentist holding a small round mirror near her molars. And if her housemate hadn't let this person in, then Annie would be there instead of hiding under the table. And now her housemate and her too-hopeful acquaintance are in the room, both wondering where Annie is, wondering if she is okay.

Treedaughter

Nuala Ní Chonchúir

She is a tree, this branch-haired woman with a trunk body and bark cloak. Birds nestle in her hair. At laying time, Treewoman opens her bellydoor and a partridge flies in. Treewoman closes the door and, while the bird settles, she whispers egglore to her daughter.

'Witches live in eggshells and make boats out of them,' she says. 'They brew seastorms from their shellboats.'

The treedaughter huddles closer to her mother; she does not like witches. The partridge burbles and preens.

'An egg broken in a vineyard will protect the vines from hail.'

The daughter imagines clusters of grapes, fat with wine. She sees herself break an egg and when the gloop of it hits the clay, hailstones shoot back up into the sky and melt away.

'Do not eat the bluebird's egg,' her mother says, 'it will make you love to wander.'

The daughter sees herself pull up her roots and walk out of the forest; the other trees encourage her steps. But what is there to see in the bigworld but humans and their atrocities: fire, smoke and machines? She does not think she will swallow a bluebird egg.

'If you eat a mockingbird's egg, you will tell everything you know.'

Treedaughter pictures the egg: it is blue, freckled with brown. Does she know enough of anything to tell, she wonders, never mind everything? The mockingbird may keep her egg.

'Do not eat an owl's egg or you will always shriek.'

Treedaughter likes to shriek but she does not want to sound like an owl forevermore. She likes her own noises: the squelch of root-taking, branchsnap, gentle bud-blossoming and leafrustle.

'If you eat a dove's egg, bad luck will come,' her mother says.

Treedaughter does not like doves; they sit in canoodling pairs on her branches. She shakes them off but they return and twitch their collared throats, applepip eyes flitting. They are the silliest of birds; she would not like their silly eggs.

'Do not eat the egg of any bird with yellow feathers: you will catch a fever.'

Those yellowfeathers might bring an ugly illness: leaf rot, bark canker or some such. There will be no saffron finch, canary or kiskadee egg for me, Treedaughter thinks.

Treewoman tickles her daughter with a twig. 'If you eat a crow's egg, you will laugh foolishly, ha-ha-ha.'

Treedaughter giggles. 'I toss crows from me when they land on my branches; I do not want their untidy nests matted in my hair.'

'You are wise, daughter. And, because you are such a clever sapling, you will know too that if you eat a partridge egg, you will thrive and grow.'

Treewoman opens the door to her belly and the partridge flies out, calling rick-rick-rick. In the nest is an egg, grey speckled like stone. Treedaughter cracks the egg and lets the warm albumen and yolk slip down her throat. Already she feels her branches strengthen and elongate, reaching for the time when she too will be a treewoman.

A Handful
Tim Stevenson

I thought he'd been in the river for a year, down amongst the roots and tumbling stones.

My mother told me otherwise.

On a bookshelf something remained.

She'd taken it from the crematorium, she said, and he's as useful around the house now as he ever was alive.

I wondered about the jar of grey ashes, which bit of him hadn't made it to the river: an ear, a nose, the hand that clenched his pipe?

Incomplete, my father flows away, and somewhere a fisherman eats his catch, picks grit from his teeth and thinks, inexplicably, about tobacco.

Spinning
Oliver Barton

On Monday, Maisie started spinning. Not wool, but round and round. At coffee time, I said 'I'll not offer you a cup. You'll spill it.' She said 'It was them Dervishes set me off.' How she didn't come over all dizzy, I just don't know. At lunchtime, she stopped. Suddenly. And the world started spinning in the other direction, faster and faster. Everyone was sucked off in a gigantic cyclone, like down a cosmic plughole. Except Maisie, because she'd fallen over, and me, because I'd screwed my feet to the floor. You want to watch out for spin.

X
Amy Mackelden

I live with every one of my ex-boyfriends. Stephen spends his time on the sofa, eating milk-less cereal and deleting my shows from the Sky box. Ted stays in the bedroom. Not to fuck, he just likes sleeping. Tim cooks, endlessly; mostly lasagne. Rob posts notes through the letterbox: Are you home? Are they gone yet? When am I getting a key? David reads Nietzsche in the armchair and Jack smokes in the tub, using my soap where he shouldn't.

Mum likes them all, and Dad says, 'No rush. Like laptops and hard drives, it's good to keep a back-up.'

Lost For Words
Andrea Mullaney

When I was seven, my cousin Karin told me that words had a limit. You could only say each one a certain number of times – she couldn't remember how many, exactly – and then they ran out and you couldn't ever use it again. You would open your mouth but nothing would come out. I spent a week trying to find different ways of saying the most common words, like 'and' and 'the' and 'it,' terrified of being left speechless. Then my mum noticed and told me that Karin was only kidding. The relief I felt was – was –

Oh. Oh, no.

My Grandad was Roy Rogers
Anouska Huggins

My grandad was Roy Rogers.

Except without the horse.

But he did have a Dralon armchair, the same colour as a golden palomino. He galloped on the edge of it, to keep in time with Trigger, blowing smoke from the barrel of his fingertips, while his loosened braces, like a bridle, flanked his hips. Then he'd throw off his fake buckskin hat. It smelled of Brylcreem and the oil from his old motorbike and sidecar: the one that kapooshed louder than a six-shooter.

'Here, Bullet,' he would yodel.

But the dog would just ignore him. It only answered to Shep.

Dot-to-Dot Man
Alison Wells

It was about midday last Saturday I saw this dot-to-dot man. Lucky for him the wife had asked me to whitewash over the graffiti on the front wall or I might never have seen him. Lucky I always put a pencil behind my ear for odd jobs.

His dots were numbered so it was easy to fill in the gaps. I got my pencil and joined him all together – 'though there was a tricky double back between fourteen and seventeen. When I got to the last number he went off on his way and I went back to my painting.

Slather

Clare Kirwan

Even after a week of frying our startled nipples under the merciless sun, Madeleine was still going on about how important it was to protect yourself even on cloudy days, even when the wind is cool, and how we should all be slathering ourselves in Factor 30 the way she did, greasing every inch of herself until you could practically smell her coming along the beach without opening your eyes – so it was ironic really that when the waves pulled her down a third time and everyone reached for her pale, flailing limbs, she just slipped through our fingers.

The Gradual Discovery of Loss

Eva Holland

It was her shoes that I found first. They were waiting patiently on the stairs, the left a step higher than the right, as if they had simply slipped from her feet as she ran. I took off my shoes and set them beside hers. Next I found her dress: a lake of silk on the bathroom floor. I took my clothes off and dropped them on top of it. Lastly, I found the imprint of her body on the surface of our bed. I lay down where she had lain, fitting my limbs into the hollows of her absence.

All Light
Alan Beard

The boy on the beach has his eyes closed and the chatter eddies at his ears. He thinks he's her boy-trap. He makes her sticky. The beach is rolling, the beach is swollen. Sea's froth breaks on bodies like music. I am a gull's cry. I am grass in the dunes. He's the sharpness, he's the light. Radio voices, he's a transmitter. She is a voice from a long way off and the colours brim through his opening lids, like all light trying to get in.

India
Joanna Campbell

Gracie and me know when our Mam's sad.

'Shall we make tea?' Gracie's voice is like pan-pipes in a wood.

Mam hurts Gracie so much she can't cry. Just sinks down in the corner. There's a tea-stain the shape of a melting India on the wall. She traces it with her finger.

Mam leans against the back-door jamb with her cigarette.

We'll creep under the bed, to India. Red-hot, golden and cinnamon-spiced.

Except Gracie can't come, can she?

I'll lay strings of daisies tomorrow.

She kisses my bruises, those she can reach. Goodnight, Gracie. Thank you for holding me.

Author Information List

We don't have enough room in a volume such as this to list a full biography for all of our authors, and anyway, we don't have to when they have all already done the job for us on their blogs and websites.

So, below, please find a list of the places on the World-Wide Web where you can follow up the authors from this anthology. Please read their other work, buy their books, and generally support them. That way they can continue to bring you wonderful stories like the ones you've just read.

Jenny Adamthwaite	jadamthwaite.co.uk
Jenn Ashworth	jennashworth.co.uk
Oliver Barton	musicolib.net
Alan Beard	alanbeard.net
Natalie Bowers	nataliebowers.org
Cathy Bryant	cathybryant.co.uk
Joanna Campbell	joanna-campbell.com
Nuala Ní Chonchúir	nualanichonchuir.com
James Coates	@Brev_
Claire Collison	@clairecollison1
Chris Connolly	sidecartel.com/artists
L.A. Craig	lacraig.co.uk
Judy Darley	SkyLightRain.com
Ariel Dawn	facebook.com/arielsdawn
Vanessa Gebbie	vanessagebbie.com
Kylie Grant	@KylieGrant1
David Gullen	davidgullen.com
David Hartley	davidhartleywriter.blogspot.com
Kevlin Henney	asemantic.net
Tania Hershman	taniahershman.com
Sarah Hilary	sarah-crawl-space.blogspot.co.uk
H Anthony Hildebrand	hahildebrand.com
Eva Holland	@HollandEva
Holly Howitt	hollyhowitt.com
Thaddeus Howze	hubcityblues.com

Anouska Huggins	@NooshHugg
Claire Ibarra	claireibarra.com
RM Kealy	@Gastronomics_ie
John Keating	thepennydreadful.org
Calum Kerr	calumkerr.co.uk
Clare Kirwan	clarekirwan.co.uk
Emma J. Lannie	garglingwithvimto.blogspot.co.uk
Cathy Lennon	@clenpen
Beverly C. Lucey	beverlylucey.blogspot.com
Amy Mackelden	july2061.com
R A Martens	@raarmar
Ana Martinez	anapirana.com
Thomas McColl	@ThomasMcColl2
Stephen McGeagh	@SJMcGeagh
Siobhán McNamara	facebook.com/siobhanmac.donegal
Freya Morris	freyamorris.blogspot.co.uk
Andrea Mullaney	andreamullaney.com
Clay Norman	herebewonder.com
John Paul O'Neill	facebook.com/farrago.poetry
Sonya Oldwin	@_supersonya
Jim O'Loughlin	uni.edu/oloughli
Amanda Oosthuizen	amandaoosthuizen.com
Jonathan Pinnock	jonathanpinnock.com
Dan Powell	danpowellfiction.com
Eabha Rose	theatreofwords.blogspot.ie
Sam Russell	@thequietscribe
Shelley Day Sclater	c/o jennybrownassociates.com
Ian Shine	@ianshine
Diane Simmons	@scooterwriter
Tim Stevenson	timjstevenson.com
Stella Turner	@stellakateT
Tracey Upchurch	traceyupchurch.com
Bart Van Goethem	bartvangoethem.tumblr.com
Alison Wells	alisonwells.wordpress.com
Brendan Way	facebook.com/DoingThingsThe-BrendanWay

(Note: @... addresses are Twitter names)

Acknowledgements

Calum Kerr :-
As ever, a collection like this does not arise in a vacuum. The first people to be mentioned must be the writers: those who entered this year's micro-fiction competition and produced the ten tiny tales that finish the anthology, and the hundreds who submitted specifically for this book. It is their writing, reading, sharing, promoting and general enthusiasm for all things flash that help National Flash-Fiction Day to be the success that it is and allow this anthology to exist.

Thanks must go to Holly Howitt for helping me to read through the submissions and winnow them down to the wonders you are holding in your hand. And especial gratitude to Amy Mackelden who administered the stories and helped with preparing them for publication, and to Tim Stevenson who took on the task of designing the cover and put up with all of my tweaks, changes, changes-back, and so on.

Thanks, as ever, to my wife, Kath, and step-son, Milo, for their support.

And finally thanks to you, dear reader, for buying this book and supporting what we do. It's all for you.

Holly Howitt :-
Firstly, my thanks to all who submitted to this anthology, whether your story was included or not. I enjoyed reading through every submission.

Thanks to Ben, for his advice and thoughts throughout this project.

And thanks to flash-fictioneers everywhere who are making this genre into something super.

Wall of Fame

This anthology was paid for by crowd funding. It was a new and exciting experience and we are incredibly grateful to all those who donated and made this book a possibility. Below is a list of these generous benefactors and we are sure that you will join us in thanking them. Thank you!

A E Peters, Adam Horovitz, Alison Wells
Andy Lavender, Angela Williams, Anna-Louise Hecks
Anouska Huggins, Carlie Lee, Carys Bray, Cath Barton
Cathy Bryant, Danielle McLaughlin, Diane Simmons
Duncan Kerr, Duncan Smith, Elaine Borthwick
Eva Lyne, Helena Mallett, Jen Hamilton-Emery
Jill Phillips, Joanne Key, Joanne Selley, Jonathan Pinnock
Judith Kerr, Karen Storey, Kevlin Henney, Kylie Grant
Laura Huntley, Martin Palmer, Ninette Hartley,
Nuala Ni Chonchuir, Patrick Prinsloo, Pauline Masurel
Pete Domican, Polly Robinson, Rachael Dunlop,
Sal Page, Sarah Logan, Sarah Salway, Sarah Snell-Pym
Shirley Golden, Stella Turner, Susi Holliday,
Tim Stevenson, Tracey Upchurch, Vanessa Gebbie
Waseem Hussain, and William Kelly.

Jawbreakers

Jawbreakers, the anthology from National Flash-Fiction Day 2012 is still available.

Beautiful. Overwhelmingly brief.
Wonderful. Epically quick.
Perfect. Massively short.
In the time it takes to drink a glass of water, they balance a world on your tongue.
Matt Shoard—*Fleeting Magazine*

Jawbreakers is a total treat.
This exhilarating collection
of flash fiction, will leave you breathless
and gasping for more...
Frances Everitt—*Bridport Prize*

More details about this, and all things
National Flash-Fiction Day can be found at
www.nationalflashfictionday.co.uk.